BRETT SEEGMILLER

Yonder Worlds

SHORT STORY COLLECTION VOLUME I
THE FINAL GENESIS & THE DEVIL'S RUN

SEEGMILLER PUBLISHING

BRETT SEEGMILLER

The Final Genesis

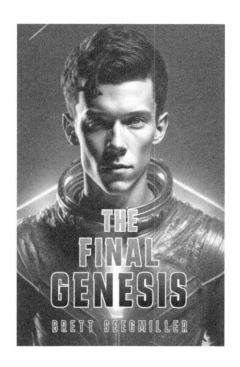

SEEGMILLER
PUBLISHING

Contents

1

Doubts in the Void

Michael felt as empty as the deep blackness that expanded into infinity before him. But even the dreary nothingness of space had stars to break up the dark. Michael had only himself. *And STAN, of course,* he thought with a frown. *But STAN hardly counts. He is nothing more than a time clock with a voice.*

Michael was three days over his fifteenth birthday, at least according to STAN's form of reckoning. It seemed unusual to Michael that a so-called year comprised three hundred sixty-five days. *What an odd number,* he thought. *Mathematics is governed by denominators of tens, hundreds, and thousands, so why three hundred and sixty-five?* It was another mystery he couldn't answer. Michael hated not having answers. A question without an answer seemed wrong somehow.

The only thing he knew for sure was that he was traveling to a planet called Newerth.278. It was what STAN called the Genesis Mission. It was the one thing besides Michael's routine schedule that STAN always emphasized. *Your mission is to travel to Newerth.278 as directed by the Formers,* STAN would always say. Whenever Michael asked for clarification, STAN never said anything more, never shedding more light on the subject, much to Michael's dismay. *Who are the Formers? What is so special about Newerth.278?*

Michael had always lived on the Genesis vessel, raised by STAN and his educational module, which focused on mathematics, chemistry, language, and agriculture. He had never known anything else. This was his life, his home. But Michael yearned for more. But he was here, and there was nothing that he could change. *For now.*

Michael leaned forward and bumped his forehead against the thick window pane that separated him from the empty vacuum beyond. He looked out at the shimmering lights that nimbly twinkled in the diSTANce. To Michael, the glass was more than a circle-shaped window. It was a door to a galaxy of unreachable knowledge. *What mysteries lie beyond my reach?* he wondered. *What wonders?* The darkness pulled him in like it was trying to unfold its mysteries and unsolvable phenomena. Michael felt like he could almost tap into the elusive well of knowledge he knew he couldn't quite reach. *Why do I feel so empty? Is that the purpose of life, to feel nothing? Why do I feel like I'm stuck in a paradox?*

"Michael," a voice said from behind, "it is time."

Michael whipped around, the mechanical voice shattering his peace. "STAN, I told you not to sneak up on me like that anymore," he said irritably.

"Whether you were startled or not makes no difference to the fact that it is time for your pre-sleep routine, Michael." STAN rolled forward. The robot's body was a perfect sphere that rolled along the white floor like an oversized marble, making a slight hum along the plastic surface. STAN's shell was a glimmering stainless steel that reflected the white surface around him. Dotted along STAN's metal surface were small portholes with long tentacle-like arms stored inside. Michael had only seen STAN use the arms when he was helping Michael with his gardening. Aside from those specific circumSTANces, STAN always just kept to his spherical appearance.

"Yes," Michael replied to STAN's almost sarcastic quip about his routine, "but I am no longer a child, as you generously point out every year. I am fifteen years old, you know."

"Fifteen years and three days," STAN corrected.

"I know the days," Michael replied. "But somehow ... days are becoming less important. It's almost as if they move quicker."

"Time does not change, Michael," STAN replied, slowly lulling around in a small circle on the ground.

2

"Time may not change, but my *perception* of time does," Michael said. "The older I get, the more days seem to meld together, like they don't mean anything anymore." Michael looked down at the round robot at his feet. "Do you ever feel that way?"

"I am incapable of feeling," STAN replied. "It is time for your pre-sleep ... "

As STAN talked, a sudden urge not to perform his pre-sleep routine overcame Michael. He was usually strictly obedient, but he was feeling uncharacteristically rebellious and inquisitive. *STAN has to know more than he lets on.* "How old are you, STAN?" Michael quickly asked, interrupting STAN's command.

"I cannot respond to that inquiry," STAN replied.

Michael frowned. "You *cannot*, or you *will* not?"

"I will not because I cannot. I cannot because I will not. My programming restricts me from responding to certain questions," STAN responded. "If I can answer your question, I am required to do so, but I am limited in how I respond. It is time for your pre-sleep routine, Michael."

Michael ignored STAN's command once more. "Who created you, STAN?"

"The Formers."

Michael paused. "Who are the Formers?"

"I cannot respond to that inquiry."

Michael shook his head in frustration. He had to know more. *There has to be more!* "Are there questions I have not yet asked that you *can* answer?"

"Yes," STAN replied.

"Can you tell me which questions I have not yet asked?"

"No."

"Why?" Michael snapped.

"I cannot respond ... "

"Yes, I know!" Michael interrupted, growing agitated. "When will we arrive at Newerth.278?"

"I cannot respond to that inquiry."

"Do *you* know when we will arrive?" Michael asked curtly. "And you just can't tell me?"

"Yes."

Michael sighed. *This isn't getting me anywhere.* He wanted to continue asking questions, but he knew that STAN couldn't answer them. Not the important questions anyway. *What does he know but can't tell me?* he thought. *What is the purpose? Why would the Formers program a machine to have knowledge it couldn't divulge to its only human passenger?* It didn't make any sense. Nothing did. "I'm going to bed, STAN."

"It is now past your pre-sleep routine," STAN replied without emotion. "Shower, brush your—"

"I know the routine, STAN. I don't need you telling me what to do every pre-sleep."

"I am here to help, Michael."

Michael looked down once more at the cold machine with a frown. "You're a machine, STAN, so you can't understand that sometimes I don't want your help."

"I will continue serving my function, whether you appreciate it or not," STAN replied.

Michael's frown deepened as he walked away, leaving STAN behind. He glanced back at the large window and the space beyond. *Someday.*

2

Sounds and Echoes

ichael quickly finished his pre-sleep routine as instructed. He showered, brushed his teeth, and cut his nails. It was the same routine every pre-sleep. Day after day. Year by year. Nothing changed but his age and a growing sense of curiosity.

Before he left the shower room, he looked at the small mirror above the silver sink to see himself staring back with cold, blue eyes. Michael liked to look at his eyes like they were some strange attraction. He was not vain; he had nothing else to compare himself to, but he looked at them because they were the only blue thing on the entire ship. Everything else consisted of shades of white or silver.

Michael's hair was a sandy blonde that he always cut short every fourteen days, or according to STAN, every two weeks. *More odd numbers.* He left the shower room and strode down the white hallway. The dim lights overhead made him realize how tired he really was. But even with the fatigue, he was still upset. He wasn't angry at STAN. He knew that STAN couldn't be changed. *But why is there so much missing?* He frowned as he thought. *Something is missing ... isn't there?*

He moved through the open archway to his sleeping quarters. The only piece of furniture that occupied the space was a small cot with white sheets. Michael walked forward, pulled the sheets up, and slid underneath. He squirmed in and leaned his back up against the white wall. He couldn't stop thinking about his conversation with STAN. There had to be answers. The Formers must have had some purpose, some design. *So why the secrecy? What had they to gain from my isolation?* he wondered. *There has to be more!* In a sudden burst of anger, he whipped his head back and hit it against the steel wall behind him. A sharp *thud* reverberated through the room. He leaned his head down and closed his eyes, his mood growing calm once more. *My habitat is nothing more than a prison.*

Sitting there, he looked up when he heard a soft *tap.* The sound was so faint Michael thought he may have imagined it. The Genesis vessel was well built; it usually did not make creaking noises or generate strange sounds unless it happened to hit a stray meteor in a meteor belt. *Could that be it?* he wondered. *Nothing more than a meteor?*

With curiosity sparking in Michael's eyes, he threw the covers off his legs and turned to kneel, facing the blank wall. He reached up with his right hand and hesitated before banging it against the wall, striking it twice. *Thud, thud.*

He waited. Seconds passed, which felt like hours. Still nothing. He was about to sink into his bed with disappointment when he heard something else. *Tap, tap.*

Michael smiled with surprise. *What is happening? It can't be STAN. What else could it be?* He hit the wall again. *Thud, thud, thud.*

A few agonizing moments came and went as Michael stared at the wall in anticipation and slight desperation.

Tap, tap, tap.

Michael's grin grew. *That can't be a coincidence! Something is making that noise.*

Michael turned abruptly when he heard the faint whirring sound of STAN approaching from one of the tunnels STAN used to get from one room to another. He couldn't be sure if he could trust STAN with the strange tapping sounds. *Best to keep it a secret for now.* He jumped under the covers and threw them over his head just as STAN rolled through a small tube-like opening in the wall near the floor. Similar passageways were all around the living and study quarters, allowing STAN to travel from place to place with ease and speed.

"Michael, is everything all right?" STAN asked, rolling out of the passageway like a train emerging from a tunnel.

"Yes, everything is all right," Michael replied, trying to keep his voice steady.

"Were you hitting the wall with your hand, Michael?"

Michael paused. "Yes. I was ... angry.

"Physical outbursts can be a byproduct of anger, Michael. Anger is a negative emotion that you must learn to control."

"Do you know what anger feels like?" Michael asked.

"No," STAN replied.

"Then don't tell me how to control my anger," Michael said with a frown.

"You assume that because I cannot *feel* anger, I cannot understand it," STAN replied. "Anger, unchecked, can ruin a human being. You must control it, or negative consequences will follow." STAN paused. "It is twelve minutes after your regular sleeping hours. Go to sleep, Michael." STAN backed up the way he came, disappearing through the darkened tunnel, leaving Michael alone once more.

Michael slowly lowered himself into his bed and wrapped the sheets over his body, leaving his shocked eyes uncovered. "Off," he said quietly. The lights dimmed and then went black, enclosing Michael in pure darkness. But he did not sleep.

Michael's thoughts raced as he thought about the strange sounds that came through the wall. *It was a communication,* he thought. *Something made those sounds.* His mind was so excited he couldn't even close his eyes to sleep. They remained open as he thought about the possibilities.

3

Cloaked Corridors

The following morning, Michael woke with a jolt when the lights turned on. Like a machine, he resumed his post-sleep routine as usual, but his mind was far elsewhere. Even though he went through the motions of showering, brushing his teeth, and grooming himself, he was distant from the menial, daily tasks. The strange sounds that had occurred precisely eight hours and thirty-five minutes ago still pressed into his thoughts like a deep nightmare. *If STAN didn't make the sounds, they must have come from inside the ship.* Michael's lips tightened as he pondered. *But where? I know the layout of the living quarters more thoroughly than simple mathematics.*

He started when he heard STAN speak abruptly from behind.

"Greetings, Michael," STAN said as he rolled up from behind. "How did you sleep?"

Michael had hardly slept at all. He guessed that he only got about three hours of sleep. "Fine," he replied, trying to sound as normal as possible.

"I'm pleased to hear it," STAN said.

Michael turned. "I thought you couldn't feel emotion, STAN. Being *pleased* is an emotion."

"Correct," STAN confirmed. "However, I am programmed with common speech phrases for increased communication."

"I see ... " Michael said, throwing the towel he had used to wipe his face over his shoulder. "I'm going to go eat my first meal now."

"I'll check on you during your study routine," STAN said, rolling into the nearby hole in the wall.

"As always," Michael said as he watched STAN slide into the dark entranceway and disappear. Michael's eyes narrowed as he eyed the strange opening, his curiosity sparking. He had never given STAN's doorways a second thought, but now ....

He got down on all fours, crawled to the edge of the open doorway, and peered inside. There were no lights in the hollow shaft, leaving it completely dark. The entrance was a little less than two by two feet, just enough room for STAN to slide through with ease, but slightly too small for Michael to fit his shoulders through. *Maybe if I took my clothes off, I might fit.* He put his shoulders to the opening and poked his head inside the dark space. *Almost enough room!* he thought as he pushed himself forward. *But I wouldn't get very far, even without clothes, before I would get stuck in the tunnel.* Michael stood to his feet and shook his head. *It will almost work ....*

Almost.

4

A Mind Adrift

The rest of the day was a blur. Michael went to the study, a circular room with a large touch panel in the center. He went through his daily studies half-heartedly, trying to stay focused but not being able to fully take his mind off of the tapping sounds and STAN's mysterious doorways.

He took his regular courses in advanced algebra, calculus, physics, chemistry, and English without any trouble. Once he was finished, he had his second meal, a plate of fruits, nuts, and vegetables he had gathered from his last harvest from the greenhouse. Once he had eaten the food on his plate, he gulped down the last bit of filtered water in his plastic cup and then went to the greenhouse and gardened for four hours. The greenhouse was a large, dome-shaped room with sun plates on the ceiling that simulated solar light during Michael's sleeping hours. During Michael's study routine, the sprinklers watered the plants, which kept the room continuously humid.

Michael liked to garden. It usually helped him focus, and today was no different. The feeling of the rough dirt between his fingertips always took his mind off of the mental pressure from his studies, putting him in a calm, cathartic state. *There has to be some way to get through those tunnels*, he thought as he pruned a large apple tree. *But how? If I try to squeeze through, I'll get stuck, and then STAN will find out what I was doing. He'll know everything.*

No answer came. As usual, Michael went about his pre-sleep routine when the day was done, quickly going through the motions. As he drifted to sleep under the comfort of his sheets, he looked up at the white wall above him that had sent the tapping sounds to him from a seemingly different world.

5

Shower Thoughts

Michael reached for the bottle that contained his hair-cleaning gel. He squeezed a glob into his hand and began rubbing it through his wet hair as the stream of water from the showerhead splashed against his naked body. The cold water felt refreshing against his skin, sending blood rushing to his internal organs as the pores in his skin tightened. He didn't even shiver. There was no hot water aboard the Genesis vessel, which Michael had grown used to.

Next, he took the second bottle of body wash and smeared the odorless paste across his wet skin.

Michael cleaned mechanically, his eyes narrow. He still hadn't come up with a solution to discover the source of the tapping noises. *There has to be a way to fit through STAN's tunnels,* he thought. *Where does STAN go when I'm studying and gardening?* As he placed the bottle back onto the shower rack, the bottle slipped out of his hand and fell into the puddle around his feet. Michael had to steady himself as he reached down and picked the bottle off the shower floor. He looked at it steadily for a moment as an idea formulated in his mind. *The bottle was slippery from the wash on my hands.* Michael's eyes brightened. He had a plan.

6

Tunnel of Uncertainty

"I'm glad to see you've already started," STAN said as the machine rolled up from behind.

Michael was already sitting at his desk, trying to keep his arms from trembling as adrenaline coursed through his body. "I thought I would get a jump start on things today," he replied, trying to keep his voice casual.

"Very good," STAN replied as the machine began to roll away.

"STAN?" Michael asked, turning in his seat.

The robot stopped immediately. "Yes, Michael?"

"Where do you go while I study and garden?" Michael asked. He had to put a substantial amount of concentration into keeping his voice even.

"I perform routine maintenance duties," STAN replied. "Is that all?"

Michael kept his face taut. "Yes, that's all." When STAN disappeared through the dark tunnel, Michael let out his held-in breath and relaxed. *Routine maintenance?* he thought. *Not a chance.*

He waited a full minute to ensure STAN was completely gone before he bolted to his feet and rushed for the bathroom. His breath quickened as excitement overtook him. What would he find on the other side of the tunnel if he made it through? What possibilities?

He couldn't help but grin as he bolted into the shower, grabbed the bottle of body gel from the rack, and rushed outside. He already had his small knapsack waiting for him by the sink. He removed his white jacket and continued to undress, quickly folding each parcel of clothing and stuffing them into his bag. Once completely naked, he put the bag on the ground, removed a cord of twine he had brought from the greenhouse, and tied one end of the string to the strap on the bag and the other to his ankle. This would allow him to drag the pack behind him through the tunnel. Lastly, he gripped the bottle of body gel and began smearing the smooth substance evenly across his body, turning himself into a slippery mess.

Once the task was complete, he lowered himself so he was lying prone on his stomach, his eyes searching the black hole that stretched out into pure darkness before him. He wiped his forehead with his wrist as he began to sweat, not from the temperature but from nervousness. *I have to find what's out there!* He had never experienced this mixture of elation and trepidation together before. The feeling almost made him feel sick inside, but his innate sense of curiosity and adventure was the stronger force, the force that refused to let him give up and quit.

After breathing in a few heavy breaths, he plunged forward. He pulled himself up to the mouth of the tunnel and squeezed his shoulders through the opening. His eyes glinted with satisfaction as the body gel allowed his slippery shoulders to wiggle through until his entire body was encompassed in the confines of the narrow tunnel. *Push!* he commanded himself.

He wriggled and spun, using the palms of his hands to pull himself forward into the hollow space. Michael still had the bottle of body gel in front of him that he pushed forward so he could use it to lubricate the tunnel around him if he happened to get stuck. But so far, his body was slippery enough that he could push onward at a reasonably good rate, considering the circumstances. The cord attached to his left ankle pulled the knapsack behind him, which contained his clothing so that he could redress on the other side.

If he made it.

Adrenaline pulsed through his body, his excitement rising as he continued to move into the dark abyss. He could only think about moving forward and the possibilities ahead. He was crawling through total darkness now and couldn't see anything in front of him. He could only reach forward and feel the cold steel panels encapsulating him as he continued pulling himself through. He could tell that after slithering along for some time, the tunnel curved in different directions like a squiggly line on a piece of paper.

But then, after traveling for a few minutes, he felt something he didn't expect, something utterly foreign to him. Claustrophobia.

Terror seized him as his sense of adventure disappeared like a wisp of smoke, his body realizing it was constricted unnaturally. Gone was the simple luxury of stretching and moving his body around in free space. He had previously felt confined in his living quarters, but this was true mental and physical imprisonment. He began to panic, but he frantically tried to push himself forward. Darkness surrounded him in all directions. There was no way out, no release from the cold steel that seemed to be digesting him like a metal organ.

I'm going to die! he thought. *Why did I do this to myself? I'm going to die, and STAN won't be here to help me.* Sheer madness pushed him forward. He clawed and scraped at the steel panels around him in a blind fury. He was about to give up and accept his fate when he saw a small glimmer of light ahead of him. He stopped to squint at the strange sight. It had felt like hours, days, even since he had last seen the comforting glow of orange light.

Michael's face hardened. Determination overcame his sense of fear as he made one final lunge forward. He must have almost blacked out because he could barely recall how much time it took to free himself from the black tunnel, from the cold clutches of dark death.

7

The Awakening

Michael quickly dressed, but his thoughts were racing faster than his trembling hands. He found himself inside another bathroom almost completely identical to his own, even though there was something ... *off* about it. It took him a moment to realize what the difference was exactly. *It's backward,* he realized. He looked around anxiously as he pulled his shirt down over his head. After shrugging on his white jacket, he put the bottle of body gel into his knapsack. Cautiously, he backed up against the wall into the shadows as he slung the bag over his shoulder. He was no fool. Anything or *anyone* could be wandering these halls, even STAN. *Especially STAN,* he thought with a frown. He wasn't sure how STAN would react if he found Michael outside his living quarters, but he wasn't in any hurry to find out. *I've gotten this far. Now is not the time to get careless.*

He slowly crept down the familiar but reverse hallway that took him past the study room. He slowly peeked around the corner. Nothing. He continued.

Next, Michael came to the kitchen. There was still no sign of anybody. He quietly walked into the room, moved around the eating table, and into the greenhouse. The dome-shaped room was exactly the same as his own, save for the plants themselves. Michael moved into the center of the dome and looked around. The same plants and trees grew all around in a bustle of greenery, but the arrangements were vastly different. Michael kept his plants bunched together in semi-neat squares, but the plants in this green room were lined up in meticulously lined rows, separated by each type of plant. He smiled as he looked around. Whoever lived here was a person just like him, albeit slightly more organized. *There's just one last place to look.*

He slowly walked out of the green room and went down the dimly lit hallway again until he came to the sleeping quarters. The open archway was dark and quiet. Michael planted his back up against the wall next to the doorway, his body going tight in anticipation. He inhaled a deep, careful breath. *What is in there? Why am I still afraid?* He wasn't sure what to be scared about, but he was still filled with anxiety and dread. Adrenaline began pumping through his body as he prepared to greet what was beyond the threshold.

Get it over with! his mind screamed. Michael whipped around the corner as a figure in the bed shot up. Michael stared in horror as the person in the bed began to scream.

8

Vanishing Act

M ichael shot forward in a lunge as the figure in the bed continued its blood-curdling scream. He jumped up on the bed, pushed the figure down, and quickly clamped his hand over the person's open mouth, effectively muffling the scream. The person tried to kick and bite, but Michael held firm as he looked out the doorway and listened. The figure beneath him continued to struggle as Michael strained to hear if STAN or something else had heard the scream that seemed like it was still echoing off the steel walls around him. After a few moments, he looked down. He could barely see anything in the dark room, but he could make out two bright eyes staring back at him in horror.

"It's all right," Michael whispered. "I'm not going to hurt you."

The person began struggling again, trying to catch Michael off guard. He leaned down and pressed harder, holding the person's flailing limbs.

"You're somebody ... someone like me," Michael continued, in hopes that talking would soften the person's retaliation. "And I'm like you. I won't hurt you."

The person beneath him relaxed, and he could see the fear in the person's face slightly fade, but not altogether.

Michael paused. "If I take my hand off your mouth, will you promise not to scream? Nod your head if you want to say 'yes.'"

The person hesitated but nodded. Slowly, Michael released his hand from the person's mouth, and as promised, no scream erupted. Michael slowly rose to his knees and stepped off the bed, letting the person sit up.

"My name is Michael," Michael interjected into the darkness after a few moments.

For a moment, the person in the bed didn't respond. As Michael was about to say something else, the silent figure spoke. "Step into the light." The voice was soft and smooth.

Michael hesitated but complied and took a few steps back so he was standing in the hallway. The dim light cast shadows across his thin face. He continued to peer into the room, only able to see the silhouette of the person inside. "What's your name?" Michael asked.

The figure rose to its feet and slowly stepped forward until Michael could see her in the dim light. She was a few inches shorter than he, with deep brown eyes and long brown hair braided behind her head.

"I'm Olivia," she said softly, carefully eyeing him like a wild animal.

"Olivia ... " Michael whispered, testing the name in his mouth. "I—" Before he had a chance to react, Olivia whipped her arm forward and released the sheet she had secretly pulled from her bed, which soared out in a wave, covering Michael's entire body which blocked his sight. Michael grunted as Olivia crashed into him from the other side of the sheet, jabbing a shoulder into his stomach. As the wind got knocked out of him, he fell back against the wall behind him, giving him a bruise on the back of his head from smashing against the steel wall.

He struggled before ripping the sheet off his body. He looked around. Olivia was gone.

9

Secret Partner

Michael shot to his feet, throwing the white sheet to the ground. He backed up against the wall as he looked down the empty hallway, the feeling of dread returning. *Where did she go?* He kept his eyes focused on the abandoned hallway. *She's going to alert STAN!* he quickly realized. *I have to stop her.*

Fear pulsed through him as he carefully made his way down the curving hallway. *I can't get caught, not now!*

He came to the door that led to the kitchen and green room and peeked around the corner. Olivia wasn't visible, but the green room was large, meaning she could be anywhere. Michael glanced in the direction of the study and bathroom. She could be in one of those rooms, possibly hiding in the shower, but it seemed more likely that she would have run to the green room where she would have more space to hide. He turned his eyes back to the kitchen and slunk forward, trying to keep as quiet as possible. He quickly located the small nooks and crannies that could make good hiding spots in the kitchen and swiftly moved on. As he emerged from the kitchen and into the green room, he dashed behind a large cherry tree covered in vivid pink leaves and hunched down beside the trunk. He slowly scanned the large dome that was bristled with diverse types of fruit trees and vegetable plants.

Nothing.

Michael dashed to another tree. He still couldn't see any sign of Olivia. *Am I wrong?* he wondered, scanning the area around him. *Perhaps—*

He fell to the ground when something hard smashed against the back of his skull. A flash of pain erupted in his head, almost knocking him unconscious. He forced himself to stay awake as he quickly spun around, so he was lying on his back, looking up. Olivia stood a few feet away with a shovel gripped tight in both hands, holding it up in a defensive position.

"Are you what made the tapping noises?" she asked sharply.

Michael groggily stumbled to his feet as he responded. "Yes, I made the tapping noises." He paused, trying to STANd steady. "And you were the one that responded to me."

She hesitated. "I knew I shouldn't have, but I—"

"—couldn't help yourself?" Michael finished.

"Yes," Olivia replied with a frown.

Michael smiled at the strange way it had felt natural to finish Olivia's sentence. "I'm like you," Michael said, spreading his hands wide to show he wasn't hiding any weapons. "This place, has it ever been enough for you? Don't you feel that something is—"

"—missing?" she said, looking up at him with wide eyes.

Michael smiled and nodded. Olivia smiled as well and was about to say something when they both heard the noise. STAN was coming.

"Quick!" Olivia said, grabbing Michael's hand. She dropped the shovel into the dirt as she rushed forward, towing Michael behind her until they came to the storage locker. "Inside!" she commanded.

Michael didn't hesitate. He flung the door open and stepped inside, joining the shovels and rakes in the cramped space. *Not again,* Michael thought as Olivia quickly closed the door, enclosing him in darkness once again.

Michael closed his eyes and forced himself to remain calm, trying to push away the fear. *Just be still,* he ordered himself. His eyes slowly began adjusting to the darkness, but he focused on the sounds around him. He could barely hear Olivia's feet as she softly moved away, her footsteps padded by the fresh dirt. He waited. As the moments dragged on, he began to fidget. He couldn't hear anything now. He strained to listen, but there wasn't any movement outside. Then suddenly, STAN began speaking.

21

"Olivia, it is four hours and twelve minutes past your sleep routine. Why are you not in bed?" STAN asked, his voice muffled by the shed door.

"I couldn't sleep," Olivia replied. "I thought that gardening might help."

STAN paused. "Does this have anything to do with the other night when you were hitting the wall?"

Olivia hesitated. "No," she replied. "I was just restless, that's all."

"Very well," STAN said, "but I must insist that you return to your bed and resume your sleep routine. I will escort you."

"Okay," Olivia said as she followed STAN out of the green room. "I am pretty tired."

Michael waited as he listened to Olivia's footsteps fade away and STAN's rolling sound disappear entirely. Even then, he waited. Michael couldn't be sure where STAN would be after the robot confirmed that Olivia was safely in her bed. Michael wasn't sure how long it had been when he reopened the door. The green room seemed darker after being stuck in the closet for so long. He slowly creeped out and listened. He quickly turned around when he heard something from behind.

"Michael?" Olivia stood ten feet away, enclosed in the shadow of the doorway, arms folded.

Michael took a deep breath. "STAN?"

"Gone," she replied quietly.

"Thank ... thank you," Michael said, taking a step forward. Oddly, he wasn't really sure what to say at this point. After so much speculation and fear, he now felt truly lost and confused.

Olivia paused before taking a few steps toward Michael. "I'm sorry."

Michael looked at her in confusion. "For what?"

"For hitting you in the hallway .... "

Michael smiled. "I suppose I deserved it."

Olivia smiled back. " ... and for hitting you with the shovel." She was only a few feet away now, looking up into Michael's eyes with a deep stare. She slowly reached forward and put her fingers against his chest. "Where did you come from?"

Michael hesitated. Where Olivia was touching him, it felt like she had set his chest on fire. He took a deep breath as he took her hand in his. "I'll show you." He led her through the kitchen and down the hallway to the bathroom. He stopped in front of the tunnel he had crawled through. Still holding Olivia's hand, he crouched and pointed through the dark hole. "I came from there," he said. "From a habitat like this one."

"You used STAN's tunnels?" she exclaimed, crouching beside him.

"I had to use shower gel to make myself slippery."

"Ew," she said. "I bet you're all sticky now."

"Uncomfortably so," he replied with a laugh. He looked back at Olivia. "I still can't believe you're alive. I thought I was the only one."

"I as well," she replied. "When I heard you tapping on the wall, I thought I was going crazy."

"Maybe we're both going crazy," Michael said. His eyes narrowed as he turned around to look at the other wall behind him. Another one of STAN's doorways lay a few feet away like a deep cavern that seemed to draw him in. *Could it be?* he thought.

Olivia's eyes followed. "Are you thinking ... ?"

Michael paused as he looked at the black hole. "Do you think it's possible?" he asked quietly.

Olivia turned to look at him. "What are you going to do?"

Michael's mouth crinkled. It was a spectacular thought. *There might be more of us.* He couldn't help but smile. For so long, he had felt trapped, enclosed by something he couldn't name. Now, he felt free. By sheer chance, he had broken through the wall of isolation that had kept him blocked from the truth. But he knew he had to be cautious. STAN was always about. Who knew what he truly did when he was away? Based on STAN's relationship with Olivia, Michael supposed that STAN checked up on Olivia, himself, and possibly others. Michael desperately wanted to dive right into the new hole and see what was on the other side, but he knew that in approximately an hour and a half, STAN would be by to check on him during his study routine. *I have to get back,* Michael thought with a frown.

"This is incredible. What if there are others like us?" Olivia whispered, voicing Michael's thoughts. "What would that mean?"

"I'm not sure," Michael replied. "But we have to know." They both stood as Michael turned to Olivia. "I have to go back." The words almost hurt. There was nothing more he wanted than to stay. "I can't risk being away for too long."

She nodded her head. "Will you come back?"

Michael nodded. "Tomorrow, at the same time."

Olivia put her hand on his shoulder with a look that implied that she still couldn't believe that he was real. "Be safe," she said. "I think STAN is starting to become suspicious of something."

Michael nodded his head. "You should go back to bed. You'll need all the rest you can get for tomorrow, so STAN doesn't suspect anything out of the ordinary."

Without another word, Olivia nodded before turning and disappearing into the hallway's shadows. Michael stood for a few moments staring after her. *Is this truly happening?* he wondered. Pushing all thoughts out of his head, he loosed the knapsack off his shoulders and removed his jacket as he prepared for the long, dark journey back to his habitat and new reality.

10

Quest of Secrets

Like a snake, Michael slowly wriggled out of the darkened tunnel. The day before, he had returned from Olivia's habitat to his own. He quickly resumed his study routine without further interruption. He had seen STAN as scheduled and tried to act as casually as possible. As far as Michael could tell, STAN didn't suspect anything. Not yet, at least. Now, he was back in Olivia's habitat once more. He had hardly been able to sleep or think straight the entire time. All he could think about was Olivia, Olivia, and the tunnel leading from her habitat to ... *someplace* else.

As he rose, he quickly dressed and moved down the hall to Olivia's room. He peeked around the corner. The room was dimly lit like before, but this time, he could see her form huddled on top of the bed with her arms wrapped around her legs. "Olivia?"

She slowly rose to her feet and walked forward. "So, I'm not actually dreaming," she said softly as she stepped into the light a few feet away from Michael.

"You should have been dreaming," Michael said with a smile. "You're supposed to be sleeping, you know. Sleep routines and all that."

Olivia smiled back. "Were you able to sleep?"

Michael shook his head. "Not one bit."

"That's what I thought," she replied as she stepped past Michael and into the hall, "so you better not lecture me about my sleeping habits."

"I wasn't lecturing," Michael said. "I was just ... commenting."

"Yes, well, you can keep your comments to yourself then," Olivia said with a smile as she walked down the hallway toward the kitchen.

"Where are you going?" Michael asked.

"Midnight snack," she replied as she twirled in a circle, flashing a quick smile.

Michael smiled back as he followed her down the hall. "It's the middle of the day for me, you know."

"Mid-day snack for you then."

They moved through the kitchen and into the green room. Olivia led him through a small grove of trees until they came to a grapevine that grew along a set of wires. The purple clusters of grapes looked large and ripe, much healthier than his were back in his own green room. Olivia picked up a gardening knife, cut a bunch of grapes off, and handed them to Michael, which he took gratefully. When she cut off her own bunch, she walked over to a large apple tree and sat down against its trunk as she plucked a grape and popped it into her mouth.

"These are delicious," Michael said with a mouthful of grapes as he sat against another tree so he and Olivia faced each other.

"I didn't know you could *not* grow delicious grapes," she replied.

"Well ... you can," Michael said with a laugh. "Obviously you're a better gardener than I am."

"Remind me never to visit your habitat, then," Olivia replied. "I love fresh fruit."

They sat silently for a few minutes as they finished their grapes. Michael began to feel anxious the longer they sat. He felt good spending time with Olivia, but there was something else gnawing at him. *Where does the other tunnel lead?*

"You're thinking about the tunnel, aren't you?" Olivia said, breaking Michael's stupor.

"How did you know?"

"I just ... know," Olivia replied with a look that implied that she was confused herself. "In a way, I feel like .... " she trailed off. "Never mind. I just *know* certain things about you. You're curious and inquisitive. It's your nature."

"I think STAN would call me meddlesome."

Olivia smiled. "Yes, I believe that sums it up beautifully."

Michael smiled back. "It's just that ... I *have* to know what's out there, you know? If you're here, there has to be more, right?"

Olivia frowned. "How many others do you think there are?" she asked.

"There's no way to be sure," Michael replied. "We don't even know how large the Genesis vessel is. I used to think it was just my habitat attached to the equipment section, but now it's impossible to tell."

"Do you think this has anything to do with the Formers?" Olivia asked.

"The Formers?" Michael asked in surprise. "What do you know about them?"

"Nothing, really," Olivia said. "I thought you might."

Michael shook his head, which made him wince in pain. "STAN won't tell me anything about them. The most he's told me is that the Formers were the group who sent us on the Genesis Mission." Michael sighed as he rose to his feet. The longer he sat, the more anxious he became. It killed him to have more to explore but not know what he was searching for. "Thanks for the midnight snack," Michael said, "I should get going."

"You *should*?" Olivia asked. Michael couldn't see her face very well, but he knew she was smiling at him. "And what great power is forcing you to leave?"

Michael didn't smile back. "The unknown, Olivia."

"But *why*? Why do you have to go?" she asked.

Michael frowned. "Because ... " he paused as he tried to think of the right words, " ... there have to be answers."

"And answers will give you what exactly?"

"Truth," Michael replied. "Don't you feel more *alive* knowing that I exist?"

"Of course," Olivia replied.

"That's the reason I need to know," Michael said. "The more I understand, the more complete I feel."

"Yes, but no matter how much you learn, there will always be something you do not know," Olivia replied.

"Then I'll die trying," Michael said.

Olivia reached out and held Michael's hand in hers. "That's what worries me," she replied. "But do what you feel is right. I won't try to stop you."

Michael squeezed her hand. "I'll be back."

As he turned to leave, Olivia said, "Michael, be—"

"—safe, I know," Michael said with a smile.

As he left Olivia behind, he shook his head in frustration. Now, he felt truly torn. He wanted nothing more than to stay with Olivia so he could have someone to talk to and just *be* with. Being around her felt natural, like she had been a part of his life forever. But there was the other side of him that pushed him away with an unquenchable thirst for answers. It was the same desire that led him here in the first place. It wasn't a desire that just *went* away. *If there's more out there, I'll find it. There has to be more.*

11

A Fateful Meeting

As Michael emerged into the adjoining habitat, he again felt the same dread he had the first time he entered Olivia's habitat. Who lived here? Who had wandered these halls for so many years alone, not knowing there was more just beyond the steel walls that surrounded them like a cage?

Michael cautiously started walking forward. As he approached the study, he peeked around the corner. No one was there. He proceeded to the kitchen. Michael could hear every breath like a drum beat in his head as he drew closer. He paused when he heard a sound from around the corner. *What was that?* He edged closer until he could see around the corner. A man stood beside the counter with a knife in one hand, cutting an apple into thick slices, entirely oblivious to Michael's presence. The man was taller than Michael and had a darker complexion with deep brown eyes. Michael couldn't be sure, but the man looked like he must have been a few years older than himself.

Now, the uncertainty set in. *What should I do?* Michael thought. *Just pop out and introduce myself, or let the man find me?*

Michael liked the thought of waiting, but he couldn't wait. *Not now.* Michael slowly took another step forward and turned to face the man standing in the kitchen. The man stopped cutting, but Michael could see his eyes slowly move in Michael's direction, so Michael knew the man could see him out of his peripheral vision. Michael caught his breath as the man turned, the knife in hand.

Michael didn't know what to say, so he thought he would try something simple. "My name is Michael."

The man did not respond.

Michael stood still. There was something in the man's eyes that worried him. *Does he recognize me?* The man took a slow step forward as if he wasn't sure if what he was seeing was real.

"Don't worry, I'm real," Michael said, his confidence waning. Still, the man did not respond. The man proceeded until he was only a footstep away. The man was a few inches shorter than Michael, so he had to look up into Michael's eyes. The man continued to stare for a few moments before he spoke.

"You are real, aren't you?" the man asked.

Michael smiled with relief. "Yes, I'm—"

The man's arm whipped forward in a flash, plunging the blade into Michael's side above his hip. The air jumped out of Michael's lungs as he turned to look at the man holding the knife in his side. At first, he didn't feel anything, but then a searing pain erupted through his whole body. Michael opened his mouth to scream, but nothing came out.

"You shouldn't be here," the man seethed. "You weren't supposed to come. Why do you always do this?"

Michael was still frozen with shock. The man's words echoed in his mind. *Shouldn't be here?* Michael thought. *What does he mean?* His brain wanted to shut off and stop thinking. His whole body felt feeble as he sensed his body shutting down. The man still stood before Michael with his arm extended, a vindictive scowl across his face.

Michael's mind began darkening when a single image seemed to appear before him. He saw Olivia handing him a bunch of grapes as they sat together, having a pleasant conversation in her green room. Even though they had only met twice, Michael felt as if he had known her his whole life. It was a strange sensation, but it felt *right* being around her, with her. Now he knew that he didn't want to die and wasn't prepared for it. In a flash of energy, adrenaline began kicking in. Michael's vision brightened. He viciously shoved the man with all his power, which sent him sprawling backward. The man stumbled over the chair, which sent him crashing to the floor.

Michael didn't hesitate. He rushed down the hallway back towards the bathroom. As Michael ran, he began ripping his clothes from his body. As he pulled his shirt off over his head, he stared in horror at the large red stain that covered the front section before throwing it to the floor. Michael didn't turn when he heard a voice yelling after him.

"Michael!" the man called.

Michael's only thought was about survival. He didn't even stop to think how the man knew his name. All he could think about was getting back to his habitat.

Once all his clothes were off, he quickly plunged into STAN's tunnel at the end of the hallway. Like he had been performing this task his whole life, he began sliding through the tunnel much quicker than he had on his first attempt into Olivia's habitat. As he moved, he wasn't sure if it was dark because of the lack of light or if his vision had gone black again. He didn't know, and he didn't care. All he could think about was moving forward, farther into the abyss of darkness. Before long—he couldn't be sure how much time had passed—he saw the light of Olivia's habitat in the distance. He made one final lunge and eventually emerged onto the white floor.

His mind was going numb again, and he began to shiver as he flopped himself onto his back, staring at the dim light shining overhead. His thoughts went blank as he stared drowsily at the light that seemed to be blurring his vision. *Why do I need to move?* he thought. *I could just stay here and ....* Michael snapped his eyes open. *No! Stay awake. Don't go to sleep. You need to keep moving!* Michael slumped onto his side and looked down the hallway. He could barely see the doorway that led into Olivia's sleeping chamber. Michael strained his eyes, hoping that Olivia would emerge and save him. But no one came. Michael was about to call out when he realized something. *STAN.* He frowned as he thought. *If I spend more time here, STAN will check on me and find me missing. What then? He'll search and find me here. If he sees us, he'll know everything.* Michael fell to his back once more. *I can't get Olivia involved in this. It was my choice to come here, not hers. I can't put her in any danger. If I get back to my habitat, I can tell STAN I had an accident in the kitchen. He'll believe me. He has to believe me!* Michael rolled onto his stomach and looked down in horror at the blood pooled underneath him as he lay on his back. He almost threw up all over the floor but forced himself to keep it in. *One more tunnel to go. One more tunnel and I'll be safe.*

12

Echo of Olivia

Michael could barely stay awake as he wormed his way through the tunnel. The wound in his side had grown excruciatingly painful, almost to the point where he could no longer move without wanting to curl up in complete agony and accept his fate in the tomb of steel. When he saw the light of his habitat in the distance, he could not muster any excitement over the prospect. There was only pain and numbness. He only kept moving because his body had grown accustomed to moving forward, inch by inch, foot by slow foot. When he reached the end of the tunnel, he numbly reached outward, grasped the edge of the tunnel's entrance, and pulled himself forward. With pain shooting through his body with every movement, he slowly wiggled free of the steel trap and collapsed once more onto the ground. The floor was chilled, but it felt so *warm*, so inviting. He had made it. He was home. But he wasn't quite finished. *I need to get to the kitchen.*

He pushed himself up with one elbow and rose unsteadily to his feet. He began walking down the hallway but stopped cold when he saw a strange object sitting a dozen feet away in the middle of the hallway. Michael took a step back in surprise and shock when he recognized the object was STAN hiding in the dim shadows of the hallway, waiting like a silent sentinel. "STAN!" Michael blurted out. "What ... what are you doing here?"

Keeping perfectly still, STAN didn't respond. Michael's thoughts raced, terrified, but he didn't know what to say. Whenever he asked a question,

STAN always responded. Always. Even when asked a question that he couldn't answer directly. Michael was about to say something—*anything*—when one of STAN's steel arms shot out like a whip from its steel body. Michael barely had a chance to react before the arm's tip sailed forward like an arrow and plunged into Michael's chest. Michael looked down in shock. At first, he didn't feel anything, but he could see the arm embedded into his chest with the end poking out through his back, smeared in Michael's crimson blood. Suddenly, Michael felt an intense pain that burned like a scalding liquid. The pain was so severe that he opened his mouth to scream, but no sound came. Even the knife wound in his side couldn't compare to this.

Michael looked down at STAN, but STAN remained motionless, not saying anything. Michael's vision began to darken. Michael tried to fight it off, but the blackness was too much for him to resist. His eyes closed, and as his sight dimmed, the last thing he remembered seeing was Olivia's face.

13

Reality of Illusion

Michael woke in a deep sweat. He lurched up in a jolt and tried to calm his uncontrollable breathing. He had had the most vivid nightmare. A dream, it seemed, designed to torture his very soul, his essence of being. Michael relaxed slightly and fell back into the soft bed. He tried to remember the dream, scanning through his already-forgotten memories. And then he remembered. *The girl! What was her name? Olivia ... ?* He had dreamt that he was not alone, that there was someone else to spend the tortured minutes of his days with. But now, reality was quickly settling back into place. There was no other person. There was only STAN. *Only STAN ... he* thought with a frown.

Michael threw his legs over the side of the bed and stood. There wouldn't be much sleep, not after a dream like that. There was no terror in the pits of space compared to the nightmare. It was a horror beyond comprehension. *Why does my mind play tricks with itself like this?* he wondered. *Another mystery, another unsolved puzzle.* He slowly walked into the hallway and followed the well-tread path to the bathroom. His vision was still blurry when he approached so he couldn't see himself clearly in the mirror. He bent down and splashed water from the tap into his face. He rubbed his face with his wet hands for a few moments before grabbing the hand towel.

After drying his face with the cloth, he slowly lowered it. His eyes came into view. They were the same dark blue as they had always been. His hair was still sandy blonde, but now his hairline had receded slightly since his youth. His face looked older, somewhat more wrinkled than it had years ago. He let the cloth drop. He was now in his thirties. He tried to remember his exact age. *Thirty-two? No, thirty-three now. Thirty-three and sixty-four days exactly.* Michael frowned. Time was going by so quickly now. The days seemed to fly like there was no beginning of one day and the end of another. They all seemed as one. *Every day, I wake, eat, and study. That is all I do. That is all I've ever done.*

Michael turned and warily looked down at the small doorway that lay a few feet behind him and to his left. He half expected the tunnel to be open like it had been in the dream, but the tunnel was sealed as he knew it would be. The tunnel had always been closed since he was a child. The doorway only opened for STAN. Michael stared blankly at the door before returning to his sleeping quarters. *I'm alone. I should try to get some rest for tomorrow.*

If my mind will let me.

14

Parallel Faces

"Michael."

Michael's eyes burst open, and he lurched forward. He rubbed his eyes, trying to force himself back into reality. He looked to the right and saw STAN sitting in his doorway. "STAN?"

"Yes, Michael?"

Michael shook his head to confirm he still wasn't dreaming. "What are you doing here, STAN? It's the middle of my sleep routine."

"Yes, it is, Michael. Come with me." STAN wheeled back and began rolling down the hallway. Michael's eyes shot wide in confusion. He jumped out of his bed, throwing his sheets into the air as he followed the machine. "STAN, what's going on?" he demanded. *The strange dream, now this?*

"You're journey through space and time has come to an end, Michael," STAN replied. "The mission is nearly done."

Michael reeled at this comment. *The end of my journey? Have I finally arrived at my destination?*

STAN rolled into the study room and stopped. "There is nothing more for me to explain to you," STAN said. "Hit play on the educational module, and all the answers you seek will be answered."

STAN rolled through one of his tunnels without another word, the door sealing shut behind him. Michael stood in shocked silence. For so long, he sought answers, often wondering if he would ever arrive at his destination.

But now that the answers stood before him, blocked by the press of a key. He hesitated. *Do I really want to know what the purpose of my isolation was?* he wondered. *What if the answers are more terrible than this life of misery?* Michael shook his head to get the negative thoughts out of his head. *If there are answers, I have to know what they are.* He strode forward and hit the key. He sat down and looked up at the screen before him. A face similar to his own stared back. It was not the image of a mirror but a different version of another him.

15

Echoes of Identity

"Hello, Michael," his other self said through the educational module. Michael looked closely at the image on the screen. The man before him had the same face, hair, and piercing eyes. Yet his face seemed alien. After studying him for a few moments, Michael realized why. The man before him did not have the eyes of a confused or ignorant man. This was a man of knowledge. He was fatter than Michael's current form and had sagging eyes from long, restless nights. Michael listened intently when the man began speaking again.

"Well ... " the man began, " ... I don't really know how to start this. I suppose I'll introduce myself. My name is Michael Hollsfield. I am a professor of Biological Sciences at Stanford University. Or at least, I was. I am currently the president of a group known as the Formers."

Michael perked up at the mention of the Formers.

"To put our mission statement bluntly, the Formers is an organization created for the sole purpose of keeping the human race alive. You see, I live on a planet called Earth. Earth is a ... *complicated* place. There are governments and organizations created for the sole purpose of destroying other governments and rival organizations. This is a planet encumbered by conspiracy and chaos and, worst of all, war. After World War 4, human life became destabilized. Needless to say, we've hit a point as a race where, if we don't do something drastic, we'll cease to live. The only thing standing between extinction and prosperity is us, the Formers. And by the grace of God, we'll succeed.

"That is why we created the Genesis vessel and a certain robot called STAN, which you'll be very familiar with at this point. This was the start of our glorious mission that will take us through the untrod trails of space and time. You see, we realized that the only way to secure the safety of our race was to leave Earth and travel to a new home. A *new* Earth.

Michael stared at the screen blankly, but his mind was far from empty. There was so much to take in. His mind was racing and reeling at the new information. Michael thought that perhaps he was still dreaming. But the voice on the monitor kept talking.

"But you see, we had a slight problem. Traveling through space takes time. *Lots* of time. It would take countless lifetimes to get a human being from Earth to a new home hospitable to our specific criteria of sustainable life. We tried many different methods to make it work. We tried experiments involving cryogenic sleep, or in other words, freezing a person and then waking them once they arrived. Unfortunately, these experiments were never successful. As such, our only option left was a desperate one, but nevertheless, a successful one. As you can see, we look alike, you and I. We are not ancestors, so to speak, but something much more intimate. We are both … *Michael.*"

16

Legacy Beyond Time

"Like I said," the other Michael continued on the educational module, "other forms of effective mass space travel didn't work. We had to find another way. Our solution is a concept that will no doubt be foreign to you and possibly hard to understand. We call it cloning. To make this idea easier to comprehend, imagine if you could duplicate yourself. You take a person's genes and replicate those genes to create an exact copy of that person. When a clone dies, STAN takes the body's remains to a particular place, and then the clone of the human is made. We realized that this was the only way to get a small group of the human race from Earth to New Earth.

"As you can see, I was one of those people. It's not me traveling in the spaceship, but it is, in a way. I'm traveling to New Earth *through* you.

"Now you understand why you're so special, Michael. I am a Former, but in a very real way, so are you. There have been many *us*. You don't have my memories or knowledge, but you have my nature."

Michael leaned forward, his eyes narrowing. *I'm a clone?* he thought. He could barely process the load of new information. There was so much to take in. His attention returned to the screen when the other Michael began speaking again.

"You see, there was a large group of us who volunteered for the Genesis mission," the Michael on the screen continued. "One of those people was my sweet wife, Olivia."

Michael's face paled at the mention of the woman in his dream. *Olivia is real?* he thought. *But it was a dream!*

"Olivia is a physicist who joined the Formers alongside me. Very soon, you will have a chance to meet her. She will be your companion, and you hers. Cherish her and keep her safe. I love her as you will come to love her. Soon, you will understand.

"Another person you will soon meet is Jeremiah Harris. Jeremiah is the top computer science professor alive. The Formers wouldn't exist without Jeremiah's continued support. His financial contributions and political influence have been invaluable, to say the least. He will help you lead the colony once you are established on New Earth. STAN will be a guardian once you come to the new world, but you will have to be alert and cautious nonetheless. We don't know what dangers await you, but one thing we know, the human race will not be defeated. No matter what barriers arise, you will be able to rise above them. Not by yourself. You will need the help of those around you. As a community, you will rise triumphantly and build the world we never could.

"I'm not sure what else I can say to make you understand why we did the things we did. My only hope is that you will build a life of happiness. There will be struggles and hard times, but I know you as I know myself. My dying wish is that this mission will not end in vain. Best of luck to you, and godspeed."

The screen went black, but Michael stared at it for a long while, thinking about everything and nothing.

17

A New Earth

M ichael stared at the blue planet through the pane of glass. It was a wonderful, beautiful sight. *A world full of water,* Michael thought with wonder. *I've read about oceans and beaches, but I never thought I would ever have the chance to see one. I wonder what it's like?* The blue planet was enormous. White clouds covered the blue sphere like a soft blanket. *All that open space!* The thought was elating and terrifying. What would he do once he was on the new planet? What awaited him there? He focused on the blue world, mainly because he didn't want to think about the other things pushing on his mind's back. But try as he might, an unpleasant but persistent thought kept pushing through. *Who am I?* The thought refused to leave him be. If he was a duplicate, a so-called *clone* of the original Michael, then who was he really?

A copy?

A duplicate?

Inferior?

That was the thing that terrified him the most. The former, who called himself Michael, was a man who knew who he was. *But what about me?* Michael thought. *What am I?*

"How are you feeling, Michael?" STAN asked abruptly from behind.

Michael didn't take his eyes off the majestic sight of the blue planet. "Well enough, I suppose," Michael replied.

"Understandably, this new information is much to take in," STAN said.

Michael snorted. "How is it possible for you to understand?"

"I can't understand myself personally, but I know the science and biology behind the human brain. I can comprehend how your human chemistry interprets and decodes such events."

"Have you ever been afraid, STAN?"

"No."

Michael sighed, his warm breath fogging the cold window. "I feel fear like I never have before. Why is that?"

"It is because of what you call imagination," STAN replied. "Your ability to see beyond what you can see with your natural eyes. When the human mind is presented with a situation that it does not or is incapable of understanding, it imagines the worst scenario it can conjure and fears it. Your future is about to change, and your mind fears change because it is the unknown. You fear death; you fear the others aboard the Genesis vessel. You fear me."

Michael turned to look at STAN.

"You fear me, Michael," STAN continued, "because you cannot understand me."

"That is true," Michael said slowly. "But why bring up such a point?"

"Because you must learn to trust me," STAN replied, "as you will need to trust the others. When you learn to trust, you will learn to conquer your fear. You can trust me to fulfill my mission because I have been doing it since my beginning. You will soon learn to trust the others."

"The others?" Michael asked. "Who are they?"

"I cannot respond to that inquiry," STAN replied.

"But I already know they exist," Michael said, "there is no point in keeping it a secret any longer."

"Logic cannot change my directive," STAN said. "I am programmed and limited in what I can or cannot say."

Michael's eyebrows furrowed. *Answers are unraveling around me, but still, not everything fits ... somehow.* "STAN?"

"Yes, Michael?"

Michael decided it was time to ask STAN another question that had been nagging on his mind since the revelation from the Former named Michael. "Why is the planet called New Earth.278?"

"New Earth.278 is the designation given by the Formers."

"But why the .278? What is its significance? The Former did not mention the number in the message."

"I was not given particular knowledge of the reasons behind the number."

Michael thought he would try a different approach to crack STAN's shell of hidden answers. This time, he would ask the easy questions. "Why is it called New Earth?" A question Michael already knew the answer to, but he wanted to see what STAN's response would be.

"The planet is called New Earth, following the tradition of human settlements in uncharted territories. You traveled from Earth to a new home, a New Earth."

Michael's eyes narrowed. "But you don't know anything about the number behind the name?"

"If you are asking if it is of any particular importance, I do not know. I was not provided with such information."

Michael gave up. When he was younger, he might have tried to push STAN further, but he had difficulty keeping his mind off the blue planet. Soon, he would be free to find answers for himself. The thought made him smile. "When do we land on New Earth.278?"

"Tomorrow."

Michael smiled. He could wait one day. After all, he had already waited entire lifetimes. What more was one day?

18

Reunion with Olivia

Michael slowly stepped down the railway to the grassy field below. He looked up and saw a bright star hovering in the sky like a yellow flame heating the planet. One of the three moons was slightly visible above the distant horizon, its black surface like a mole in the sky. Michael looked down as he took the final step off the Genesis vessel, his foot landing softly on the fresh grass below him. He took his time bringing his other foot forward. Once he did and both feet were planted firmly on the new planet, Michael smiled as he scanned the area around him. They appeared to be in a meadow with a grassy green terrain surrounded by a thicket of trees. Michael took a deep breath, drinking in the fresh air and foreign smells. He closed his eyes and basked in the sunlight for a few moments, losing track of time.

Eventually, he turned. He opened his eyes and looked up at the steel machine that rose high before him. The Genesis vessel was a massive tower of steel that rose into the sky, its peak glinting in the sunlight. At the base of the metallic spear was a giant ring of white steel that circled the tower, which is the section from which Michael had emerged. As Michael inspected the white ring further, he noticed that it was broken into multiple sections. *Different habitats?* he thought. His eye strayed to the left. A figure clothed in white stood off in the distance, looking up at the tower like he had just been. Even from the distance he stood, he could tell that the figure had long brown hair that blew softly in the warm wind, which was flowing quietly through the tranquil meadow. Without fully realizing it, Michael began walking toward the white-clothed figure.

As he approached, the woman turned to look at him with unbelief, a look that Michael was sure he was reciprocating. Once he stood only a few feet away, without hesitation, he slowly reached down and took her hand in his.

"Olivia?" he asked quietly.

Olivia looked up at Michael with a deep stare that seemed oddly familiar. "Michael?"

The two stood facing each other for a long while, not saying anything more. Soon, other white-clad figures came from around the ship and cautiously approached Michael and Olivia. Michael turned, and Olivia moved to his side, still holding his hand. The other clones clustered around Michael and Olivia, looking around with a range of emotions. Some were scared, others elated. But eventually, they all turned to look at Michael.

Michael now understood. He was their leader. The fate of the colony of New Earth.278 rested in his hands.

19

Legacy of Humanity

Michael poked the bright flame with a thin branch that STAN had given him. The jab sent tiny sparks shooting into the cold air. Darkness had quickly come upon them. The weaker colonists had returned to their habitats on the Genesis vessel to spend the night. Still, most had joined him uncomfortably around the fire, drawn to the warmth. Michael understood. It was hard for most of them. For their whole lives, the only thing they had known was the comfort and security of their personal habitats, their own worlds. But now, all of that had changed. In a way, a part of Michael wanted to return to his own habitat, to sleep in his bed. But he knew he wouldn't. Being here in the wilderness felt more like home than his habitat ever had, even though he still felt a deep fear inside himself.

Michael took a quick look around. Strange faces sat around the fire, shivering quietly as they put their hands up for warmth. Some of the people were old, but most were around Michael's age, he guessed. However, a few were little more than children who looked around cautiously with bright, curious eyes. Michael smiled as he looked at them before sitting back down next to Olivia. She sat on a large, flat rock of strange red and black color. She helped wrap a blanket around his shoulders as he sat.

Michael scanned the small crowd once more. The colonists were perfectly divided between males and females, with various ethnicities. Some had white skin like himself and Olivia, but some had brown skin that ranged in varied tones. Hair colors were also diverse. Some were blonde, some black, and some reddish-orange. But the one person who drew his attention was an older man sitting a few spaces away with a light frown. His eyes were a dark pool like an abyss of darkness. Michael wasn't sure how, but he was sure that this was the man called Jeremiah. He slowly summoned the courage to say something, sending his voice into the prolonged silence.

"Jeremiah?"

The man turned to look at Michael. "How do you know my name?"

Michael shook his head. "I just ... know. My *Former* mentioned a man named Jeremiah, and I recognized that man to be you."

The man continued to stare at Michael for a long while. "My Former mentioned you as well. He claimed that you were the one who saved us."

"That was another man," Michael replied. "Another man from another world. I'm just ... me."

"Are you another man?" Jeremiah asked. "We are a history of flesh and blood. We are a trail of humanity."

Michael thought about the odd statement for a few moments. "A trail of humanity?" Michael echoed softly. "I suppose. But just because we have the same genetics as our Formers, does that make us the same?"

"Yes," Jeremiah replied firmly. "Genetics is everything. Life is our inheritance, and it would not matter if it were the Former who stood in my place or myself. We are the same."

The others had turned their heads to listen to the unusual conversation.

"I'm not so sure," Michael replied calmly. "While I agree that we have the same genetics and DNA, the Former who I saw was a different man than what I am today. Experience is what directs our future. Our surroundings and very lives shape us."

"It may *help* shape us but does not govern us," Jeremiah retorted. "We are who we are. That cannot be changed."

"Perhaps it is not one or the other," Olivia interjected, drawing everyone's eyes to her. "What if we meet somewhere in the middle? We are not the Formers themselves, but we are an alternate version of them."

"Ah, the voice of reason," Jeremiah said with a smile. "I remember that about you ... *Olivia.*"

Olivia smiled back as she moved closer to Michael.

Michael sighed. "Well, perhaps I won't make a good leader after all," he said with a laugh.

"Lack of knowledge does not bar one from being an effective leader," STAN said, slowly rolling into the middle of the group. He placed a bundle of neatly chopped wood in his metallic arms next to the fire. "Ignorance does. A good leader acknowledges when he does not know something and allows others to counsel and reason with him."

"The machine speaks the truth, which means there is hope for you yet, Michael," Jeremiah replied.

Michael smiled. "I only hope that we will be able to make a good life here, that we will be safe."

Jeremiah grunted. "For a time, we were immortal. For a time, we were Gods."

"For a time, perhaps. But we are alive now," Michael responded, "that's what matters."

Nobody said anything more for the rest of the night as they stared at the enchanting fire. Michael looked up at the sparks of orange that were floating up into the air, mingling with the white smoke. So far, there had been no signs of predatory animals. They had seen glimpses of other mammal-like creatures roaming the woods at a distance but nothing up close. No doubt, the wildlife had been frightened by the entry of the Genesis vessel.

The colony was safe for now. *I hope.*

20

Destiny's End

I t had been sixteen years since the Genesis vessel landed on New Earth.278. The colonists had flourished rapidly. After all, they had been trained to colonize a new planet for many lifetimes. They took the seeds from the ship and began planting crops, which brought food quickly. Coming together as a colony seemed like second nature after a while.

The colonists of age had paired off, and children began to be born. The first children were now almost adults. They were a true generation, not a lineage of clones and copies.

There were times of sadness, but most of the colonists led lives of simple happiness, content to grow their crops and raise their children in peace. But peace was something Michael did not have on this particular night. He knelt next to the flat rock on the outer edge of the meadow, next to the edge of the woods. Two of the three moon's lights flickered down through the night sky, softly illuminating the quiet field.

Clasped in both of Michael's fingers was Olivia's right hand. It was cold. Very cold. The coldness that only comes from death. She had died unexpectedly. A heart attack, Jeremiah had told him. There was nothing anyone could have done. Michael's eyes were that of a man lost, grieved to the point of having an aura of emotionlessness. The funeral ceremony had been simple and short. All the colonists had returned to their homes, leaving Michael alone with his three children. Billy, Mary, and Elizabeth.

"Dad?" Billy asked quietly. Billy stood resting on his hunting spear. "We should go home."

Michael did not turn. He had a hard time processing the words through his comatose brain. "No, you go. I'll stay a little longer," he replied.

"But Dad—"

"Now, son!"

Without another word, Billy led the other two away from the flat rock, their soft footfalls disappearing into the darkness. After they were gone, Michael began to cry. He didn't want them around for what he planned to do next. He looked up at Olivia's profile as she lay on her backside, her face pointing up at the darkened sky. She was beautiful, just as she had always been. She was resting on the rock they had sat together on their first night on the new planet. However, the stone had a new meaning now. It was the resting spot for the dead descendants of the Formers. Whenever a colonist died, the remaining clones laid the body on the stone, and STAN would come in the night and take the body away. No one knew why. After all, STAN hadn't been seen in many years. STAN never took away the bodies of the children born on New Earth.278. There was a separate grave for them not far to the east. To the children, STAN was a legend, a creature of the forest that wasn't real but in stories. But the colonists knew. They knew he was real. But one day, he disappeared and didn't return, only reappearing to retrieve the bodies of the dead.

Michael's scowl deepened. *But why?* he thought. *What is the purpose?* Michael looked up at Olivia's face once more. Michael did not have the answers. He had learned much since arriving on the planet, but still, he felt as ignorant as he had when he was a child under STAN's tutelage. *Did my Former not have all the answers either? It seemed like he did, but perhaps he felt as I do now. Lost, overcome.* He gritted his teeth as he prepared for the task at hand. *This time, I'm going to follow STAN and see where he takes the dead. What will he do with my sweet wife?* He couldn't help but feel like he had when he lived on the Genesis ship. He had always felt uneasy, like something was missing. While much of that feeling disappeared once they had arrived, the same sense of dread returned once STAN began taking away the dead bodies. *There is something more going on, but what?*

Michael shot to his feet when he heard a *snap* in the forest. He scanned the shady trees. STAN was coming, coming for *her*. In a flash, he ran off and hid behind a stack of lumber resting next to the carpenter's shop. This was the only place where Michael could get a clear view of the rock without anyone or anything being able to see him. He waited, carefully peeking around the side of the rough boards, trying to calm his troubled breath. A long time seemed to pass before he saw the machine.

STAN.

STAN slowly rolled forward, the moonlight reflecting off his silver frame. Michael's blood turned cold as he saw STAN's arms pop out of his silver shell before reaching for Olivia. Michael's fists clenched so hard he thought he drew blood. In the distance, STAN slowly lifted Olivia's lifeless body over itself and started moving forward.

Michael frowned. He thought that STAN would have disappeared back into the forest, but instead, STAN was moving straight for the Genesis tower located in the middle of the meadow. The Genesis vessel still stood as it once had. However, after a few days, STAN or the ship itself had sealed the doors so nobody could get back inside. Michael had thought it a very good thing at the time, but now, seeing STAN approaching the tower made him nervous. It had been a lifetime since he had lived on the ship, and he had no desire to return.

Michael turned his eyes towards the ship and saw Olivia's habitat door open, a soft yellow light spilling into the dark night from within. STAN was heading right towards it with Olivia still in his arms. After STAN wheeled up the ramp and disappeared inside, Michael bolted forward. As he approached the ramp, the door started closing from above. Michael made one last dash up the ramp and leaped forward, barely sliding under the doorway as it sealed shut behind him. Michael turned to look down the hallway and saw STAN at the end in front of the sink and mirror. It didn't appear as if STAN had heard or seen him come through. The robot sat like it was waiting for something. *Waiting for what?* Michael wondered. In a moment, the sink and mirror began to move. The different pieces slid away like cabinet doors, revealing a long, dark tunnel behind. Michael stared in awe. *So there is more!*

STAN immediately began moving forward, so he disappeared into the black tunnel, still towing Olivia's body. After Michael was sure STAN was gone, he shot to his feet and rushed forward. As he came to where the sink and mirror used to be, he looked down and saw a black tunnel the size of STAN's body. Michael recoiled in horror at the sight. The door was open. *The doorway ... it's not sealed! All the doorways in my habitat were closed!* Distantly, Michael recalled a foggy memory of a young man crawling through the dark tunnels. A boy possessed with curiosity and imagination. A boy willing to do anything for answers. A boy who had found the girl he knew he was meant to be with. A boy that STAN had killed without explanation.

Suddenly, it all came crashing down in his mind as the puzzle pieces came together. *That was the memory of another me,* he thought in horror. *STAN killed that boy to keep him ignorant of the truth. He murdered that other me, and now he's taking my wife into the ship.* Anger overcame Michael. He shot forward into the tunnel.

The steel tunnel made the air feel cold. Michael kept running forward. He had to know what STAN was doing with Olivia's body. There had to be a reason STAN would be doing this. There had to be a reason STAN had killed his previous clone, or rather, *one* of his previous clones. Just as soon as Michael felt like he could run no more, the tunnel ended, and he found himself in a large chamber with a domed ceiling. In the center of the room was a large tube with glowing blue liquid, just the perfect size to fit a grown human. STAN had set Olivia down on the cold floor and was opening the top of the glowing tube, the light dancing playfully off the domed ceiling.

"STAN!" Michael yelled.

STAN dropped the hatch and turned. "Michael? You are not supposed to be here."

"STAN, what are you doing with her?"

"I cannot respond to that inquiry, Michael. You should not be here." STAN quickly rolled around the side of the tube and rushed towards Michael in a quick dash. Michael tried to run, but STAN jumped off the ground and hit Michael in the chest like a bowling ball, knocking him to the ground.

Michael tried to regain his breath when STAN whipped out a tentacle that glinted in the soft light. Michael stared at the arm in horror. He had experienced this before, or another *him* had. He still remembered the feeling of STAN's arm sticking through his chest. Michael prepared to experience the same feeling of horror as the tentacle whipped forward. The arm caught itself in mid-strike when a voice spoke from out of the darkness.

"Stop."

Instantly, STAN recoiled its arm and returned to its spherical shape. Michael struggled to his feet to try to spot the person who had spoken. "Who are you?"

"You know who I am, Michael."

This time, Michael recognized the voice. "Jeremiah?"

To Michael's right, Jeremiah emerged from the darkness. "Hello, Michael."

"Jeremiah? What are you doing?" Michael asked.

"I am completing my destiny, Michael. The question is, what are *you* doing?"

Michael was so upset and bewildered that he could hardly speak. "I came to see what STAN was doing with my wife's body!"

"Ah, yes. *That.* Don't worry. I've allowed Olivia to live her life. It now belongs to me."

"What do you mean, Jeremiah? What is going on?" Michael paused as Jeremiah stared back at him with cold eyes. "Tell me!"

Jeremiah sighed. "I suppose it won't hurt at this point. After all the trouble you caused with our last voyage, you won't be returning with us ... this time."

"Last voyage?" Michael asked.

"It's really not that hard to understand," Jeremiah replied. "Didn't you ever wonder why this planet is called New Earth.278?"

Michael paused. "Yes ... I wondered," Michael replied slowly. "STAN told me the number didn't mean anything."

Jeremiah smiled. "He told you he didn't know the meaning of the number, but he never said it didn't mean anything. Think, Michael. Did the original Michael ever mention the number 278?"

Michael thought back to the message from the Former. "No," he finally concluded. "All he said is that we were traveling to New Earth. He never mentioned a number."

"And why do you think that is?"

"Are you saying ... " Michael began, " ... that this is not New Earth?"

Jeremiah shook his head like a frustrated parent. "I am astonished that it took you this long to figure it out. We have been to hundreds of planets, you and I, leaving a trail of descendants in our wake."

Michael took a step back like he had been punched in the chest. *Hundreds of planets?* Michael thought. "But why, Jeremiah? Why didn't we stay on the original New Earth?"

Jeremiah sighed. "Truly, you are a version of your former self. You see, your vision of the future was so narrow. You couldn't see past New Earth. You refused to give credence to the eternal implications of our discovery. To you, the cloning process was merely a means to an end."

"But you saw it as something more," Michael interjected, his words soft as he began putting the puzzle pieces together. "That is why you joined the Formers. You wanted the cloning device."

Jeremiah nodded. "Indeed."

"But why? So you could live forever?"

"The answer's not that simple. I wanted immortality, yes. But I also wanted what you refused to provide. I saw a way to find a solution to humanity."

Michael's eyes narrowed. "A solution to humanity? What are you talking about?"

"My true mission, my *purpose*, is to create the *perfect* society. The Formers believed that if we relocated to a new planet, everything would magically fall into place somehow, but life doesn't work like that, Michael. A perfect society can't simply grow; it has to be engineered. I saw what happened to Earth. I will not allow disorder to continue. Once we arrived on New Earth, I adjusted STAN's programming, so my orders would be intermingled with his original directives.

"His original programming stipulated that he would destroy the cloning device you see before you once we reached New Earth, but I altered him so he would continue the cloning process. Once all the original colonists died, STAN continued the program so I could continue my work. My clones worked to establish the perfect society that we all longed for."

Michael frowned as he listened. "If that's true, that means you've been unsuccessful," he said slowly. "You haven't been able to build the perfect society, have you? You keep failing, over and over again."

Jeremiah's eyes went cold as his face tightened. "It is true that I have as yet been unsuccessful. But in time, I will succeed."

"You think you can build the perfect society?" Michael shouted. "You can't force perfection, Jeremiah. You will never accomplish your mission until you learn to be a leader, not a conqueror." Michael paused. "If you ever managed to create the perfect society, would you stop this madness?"

"No," Jeremiah replied. "There is no end. My work will continue for the rest of eternity."

Michael shook his head in frustration. "You think you're God."

"Why not?" Jeremiah replied. "The God of old wasn't able to save us, so I stepped in to correct the situation. Anyone can be God with enough time, and time is what I've acquired. With each rebirth, I become more than I ever was before. I have become the constructor and designer." Jeremiah turned and pointed at Olivia's body lying next to the glowing tube. "If you can't understand reason, maybe you can understand this. Olivia doesn't have to die, Michael. She can live forever, traveling through the stars like an angel of time. Would you strip her of that? Would you destroy her immortality? I can *save* her."

For a moment, Michael almost felt himself softening towards Jeremiah's proposition. But as quickly as the feeling came, he pushed it aside. He wanted nothing more than to have Olivia back, but she was gone. "No, Jeremiah," Michael replied coldly. "That is not the fate I wish for her. We've all lived too much and too long. This has to stop."

Jeremiah took a step forward. "You can't stop me, Michael."

"What are you going to do? Kill me?" Michael asked.

"Possibly. It wouldn't be the first time."

Michael looked up in shock. "First time?"

"A long time ago, a clone arrived in one of my former self's habitat. I wounded him with a knife and ordered STAN to finish the rest. I then had him seal the tunnels around your habitat so you would no longer be a burden. But here you are, as much of a thorn in my side as you've always been."

Michael gritted his teeth. "Jeremiah, I can't let you continue doing this."

"I know," Jeremiah responded coldly.

Michael took a step forward so he was facing Jeremiah head-on. "If you're going to kill me, do it yourself. No tricks."

Jeremiah whipped a blade from a sheath on the back of his belt and held it up to look at the glint of light off the blade's surface. "There is no difference if I used my blade or ordered STAN to kill you. They are both weapons at my disposal."

Without hesitating, Michael bolted forward and slammed his shoulder into Jeremiah's gut, sending him sprawling to the ground before he had a chance to attack with his knife.

"STAN, stop him!" Jeremiah ordered as he tried to rise to his feet.

Michael turned around as STAN rose behind him, arms extending out of its body like a giant spider. Michael didn't have a chance to react as STAN rushed forward and sliced an arm out like a whip that cut through the skin on Michael's chest. The force of the blow knocked Michael back twenty feet as he tumbled along the steel floor. He lay gasping on the ground as Jeremiah began stumbling forward. "STAN, stop!"

STAN froze, still in its spider-like form.

Jeremiah sighed as he stepped closer. "Michael, you will never cease to be a thorn in my side. But you are right. I should kill you myself. We are, after all, *friends.*"

Michael could barely move. It felt like all the bones in his chest had been shattered.

"But I will sleep much better at night knowing you are dead." Jeremiah was holding the blade up and was about to plunge it down into Michael's chest when another figure burst out of the darkness and tackled Jeremiah to the ground. Michael forced himself to sit up to see who the new attacker was. Billy, Michael's oldest son, shot to his feet and held his spear against Jeremiah's chest.

Michael could hardly believe his eyes. *How did Billy get here?* he thought. *The door was sealed shut behind me! There was no way in.* But now was not the time to think of such things. Jeremiah and STAN were still both dangerous. If Jeremiah awoke STAN, then all would be lost.

"Billy, kill the robot!" Michael shouted.

Without hesitating, Billy turned and rushed at the frozen robot. Jeremiah turned on the ground and stretched out his hand. "No! STAN, stop him!"

In a flash, STAN awoke from his frozen state and whipped an arm out which connected with Billy's chest, sending Billy flying through the air. Billy's spear clattered to the ground ten feet from where Michael lay. Michael looked in horror at Billy's limp body on the other side of the dome. In a flash of adrenaline, Michael shot to his feet, ignoring the pain that shot through his system. He rushed forward, picked up Billy's spear in both hands and turned. Jeremiah stood before him, breathing heavily, the hand with the knife hanging at his side.

"You won't kill me, Michael," Jeremiah said with a tired look. "You can't stop me."

"No," Michael replied with a frown. "But I can stop him!" He tossed the spear up in the air, snatched it with one hand, and turned. His arm shot forward, and the spear sailed through the air like an arrow before plunging into STAN's core with a loud metallic screech that rang through the dome. Instantly, the robot fell limp and collapsed to the ground. Jeremiah looked at STAN's dead frame in horror before turning to Michael. His eyes burned like fire as he screamed in horror. "You fool! You've ruined everything!" Jeremiah raised the blade and rushed at Michael, a glint of madness in his eyes.

Michael wanted to move to defend himself but hesitated. All he could feel was the blade plunging into his side as it had happened before. As Jeremiah was only five feet away, Billy smashed into Jeremiah from the side in a blur, sending them both tumbling to the ground once again, Jeremiah's blade bouncing harmlessly onto the floor. Billy stood up as Michael rushed forward and grabbed Jeremiah by his shirt.

"Jeremiah, it's over!" Michael shouted.

Instantly, Jeremiah began sobbing uncontrollably. Michael stared at Jeremiah for a few moments before collapsing onto his back with a groan.

It's over.

Epilogue

Michael joined Billy on the flat rock next to the woods. They had already removed Olivia's body from the ship and had given her a proper burial in the grave to the east. They had left Jeremiah in the Genesis vessel for the time being. They would retrieve him on the morrow. *He will be no harm now,* Michael thought. *Without STAN, he is nothing.*

He groaned as a sharp pain flared in his chest. The spot where STAN had hit him still hurt whenever he moved, but the pain was slowly receding. Billy looked at him with concerned eyes.

"Are you all right, Dad?"

Despite everything, Michael smiled. "Yes, I think I will be. How are you doing?"

Billy grinned. "I've had worse."

The pain flared as Michael laughed. "So tell me something, Billy. How did you get onto the ship behind me? The doors were sealed shut."

Billy smiled. "The doors aren't the only way onto the ship, Father. There are other ways. I've been inside many times."

"You found a way into the ship? Why?"

Billy shrugged his shoulders. "I don't know. I was just .... "

"Curious?"

Billy smiled and nodded his head. "I overheard you and Jeremiah talking. Does that mean there are others like us?" he asked, motioning upwards toward the night sky.

Michael nodded as he looked up at the bright stars that shimmered overhead like a blanket of sparkling diamonds. "Yes, there are others like us." Michael looked down at Billy once more. "They're out there ... somewhere. Maybe someday, we'll find them."

BRETT SEEGMILLER

The Devil's Run

Contents

1

The Greenleg

Cora wasn't sure what woke her first, the explosion or the alarm. The walls quickly stopped shaking, though the lightbulb that hung by an electrical cord still swung from the ceiling. She groaned as the alarm blared outside the door. She pulled the pillow out from under her head and smothered her face with it in an attempt to muffle the noise. As much as she wanted to, she knew she couldn't go back to sleep.

A Run awaited her.

With a sigh, she threw the lumpy pillow across the small room. She rose from the cot, which squeaked underneath her weight. The electric light was still swinging from the cord above her, making the shadows come alive on the concrete walls.

Cora clumsily made her way over to the foggy mirror, which was stained with blotches of toothpaste and hard water. She had never made an effort to clean the mirror, and she was sure that no one else ever had either. It was a testament to the laziness of her predecessors. *Or maybe they just weren't around long enough to do anything about it,* she thought. As quickly as the thought entered her mind, she pushed it away. With the prospect of a Run, she knew she had to focus.

Cora turned on the faucet and leaned over to splash water on her face. The water was ice-cold, but she was used to it. They didn't have the luxury of warm water this close to the war's front. She ran wet hands through her short black hair, pushing the wild strands away from her face to reveal icy blue eyes beneath.

She met her eyes in the mirror. A scar ran from the bridge of her nose to the top of her left cheek, which made an unnatural bulge when she smiled. Because of that, she hated smiling. Smiling also reminded her of ....

Focus, Cora! Focus! she told herself, her lips tightening into a thin line. *Get going.*

She stepped away from the sink, walked over to the thick metal door, and heaved it open. The darkened tunnel on the other side of the door seemed to stretch out into eternity in both directions. Everything in the bunker was covered in matted metal, including the walls and ceiling of the corridor. It gave the interior a cold, dead feeling.

Two doors sat on the other side of the tunnel, each marked with white paint, OLC, which stood for Over-Land Couriers. While OLC was their official title, nobody called them that.

Everyone referred to the OLCs as striders, or greenlegs for those unfortunate enough to be newly enlisted.

A four-wheeled electric cart was waiting for her in the middle of the tunnel with a spinning orange light on top. The driver, Sergeant Dalley, sat leaning over the steering wheel as he stifled a yawn. Two other passengers were already seated in the back of the cart. She recognized one of the striders but not the other. The one she recognized, Soka, didn't look like much of a runner at first glance due to his lanky frame, but he had proven to be an adequate strider who could keep up with the best of them.

The other passenger she didn't recognize had short brown hair and dark skin. This identified him as a citizen of New Arnonia, the leading coalition member of the United Front Army.

Cora warily eyed the Arnonian as she hopped into the cart and sat opposite him. The Arnonian kept his eyes on the cart floor with his arms folded tightly against his chest, his hands tucked away in his armpits.

Cora glanced up when the walls shook again from another explosion. The siren was still blaring incessantly off to the side with a red flashing light.

"This everybody?" Sergeant Dalley asked, not bothering to look back at his passengers.

Neither of the three responded.

"Cheerful bunch," the Sergeant said as he released the handbrake and stomped on the gas pedal. The cart kicked forward, making Cora reach up to grab one of the hanging straps to steady herself.

The cart raced down the steel corridor as overhead lights flashed by like strobing lights. As they moved down the tunnel, the siren sound that had woken Cora up faded in the distance behind them. The three striders sat in silence for a full minute, not making eye contact before Soka finally turned to the stranger and asked, "Is this your first Run?"

The dark-skinned man didn't look up, but he nodded his head in response.

Great, a greenleg, Cora thought. *Of course, we'd have to get stuck with an untrained Arnonian on this Run.* She covertly studied the man opposite her. She guessed he was no older than twenty-five, though his worn face made it almost impossible to tell. Cora was only nineteen, but she knew that she looked older than she really was.

"Were you a soldier?" Soka asked the Arnonian.

This time, the man looked up, but once again, he just nodded.

Now that she had a chance to study him, Cora could now see that the man had the bearing of a soldier. He didn't have the body type that was considered ideal for striders. He was too broad in his shoulders and chest area. *But what is a soldier doing here?* she wondered.

Even though the OLCs were short on numbers, the dwindling number of United Front armed forces was even more desperate. *So why send a soldier to be a strider? There's nothing wrong with him. He seems perfectly—*

Just then, she noticed that the soldier seemed to be hiding his hands through his crossed arms. All at once, it became perfectly obvious.

"Were you injured?" she asked.

The Arnonian turned and locked eyes with her. He hesitantly uncrossed his arms and raised his right forearm, revealing a bandaged stump that had once housed a perfectly healthy hand. "Caught a burst of shrapnel in the battle at Lost Man's Canyon." The soldier's smooth voice made him sound more like a professor than a soldier.

"What's your name, soldier?" Soka asked.

"Damius," the soldier replied. "Major Damius Vorte." Damius resumed his previous posture, looking away from the two sitting before him.

Cora and Soka exchanged a glance. They tolerated each other just fine, but they were nowhere near friends. She had quickly learned her lesson about friendship after what had happened to *her*.

2

The Jaw

The small cart continued to cruise down the corridor. After two minutes of traveling, the tunnel opened up into a high-ceilinged chamber. On the ceiling was an enormous steel gate that would reveal the sky above when opened.

They called it the Jaw. That was primarily due to the old red paint job on the ceiling that had peeled and deteriorated over time, giving it the image of a giant bloody mouth when opened.

To their right was a massive glass window. On the other side was a large round table with a holographic map full of blinking projected images. A dozen Arnonian generals and military strategists stood around the table, pointing at sections of the map with disgruntled looks. *The Glass Room,* Cora thought.

Sergeant Dalley pulled the cart to a sudden stop, jerking Cora forward in her seat.

"Nice stop," she mumbled.

"I hope you had a pleasant ride," Dalley replied nonchalantly, ignoring Cora's comment. "Now, get out of my contribution to the war effort so I can get out of here. I hear they're serving bacon in the mess hall."

Cora slipped out of the cart and landed on a yellow platform that was flush with the steel flooring around it. After being prepped, the yellow platform would raise them up and through the Jaw.

Soka and Damius followed behind her until they were all standing on the platform. Dalley gave them a casual two-finger salute as he released the handbrake and shot away, leaving them behind as he disappeared back into the dimly lit corridor.

The three striders stood awkwardly in the middle of the empty chamber. The generals and strategists continued arguing on the other side of the glass window. After a few uncomfortable seconds of silence, a door opened, and a tall man with perfectly combed white hair emerged. Like everyone inside the Glass Room, he wore a gray and brown camouflage uniform with military boots. In his right hand, he held a stainless steel folder. Major Garnier was the OLC Correspondent, and it was his job to give the striders their mission details. He greeted the three with a forced smile. "Good morning, striders."

"Morning?" Soka asked, looking up at the ceiling. "I can never tell in this dungeon of yours."

"I've got a good one for you today," Garnier said, ignoring Soka's comment as he opened the stainless steel folder in his hand. "Today's Run is Operation: Low Trail-04."

Cora frowned, crossing her arms as a chill ran through her body. "Low Trail?"

"What's Low Trail?" Damius asked, looking back and forth at Cora and Garnier, his arms still crossed to hide his stump.

"The Devil's Trail," Soka muttered. "The Valley of Sorrows."

"Valley of Sorrows?" Damius asked with a raised eyebrow.

"I thought as an Arnonian, you would be familiar with this area," Garnier said, thumbing through the notebook in his hand.

"No, sir. I grew up in the Coedra region."

"Well, don't worry," Garnier said, glancing up. "You'll become acquainted with the terrain soon enough."

Another set of doors opened from the chamber's side, and a team of people in white uniforms emerged. preppers.

The preppers rushed forward and arranged the three striders in a line as Garnier thumbed through his notebook, pausing to scribble notes. Cora was well used to the prepping routine. She closed her eyes and raised her arms as one of the white-clad figures raised a silver tool connected to a hose and sprayed her entire body with an odorless mist that made her skin grow cold.

"What's this?" Damius asked as he raised his arms to mimic the others.

"Just relax," Soka said, eyes closed as a prepper sprayed him down as well.

"Weren't you given an orientation, son?" Garnier asked, not looking up from his folder.

"No," Damius asked. "They just dumped me outside my room and told me to wait to be picked up."

"Care to explain what's going on, Cora?" Garnier asked as he marked something in his notebook.

Cora sighed but said, "It's called Ice Skin. It's made from a compound of thernolithium and enick leaf concentrate."

Damius stared at her with raised eyebrows. "Is that supposed to mean something to me?"

"It protects you from being seen while you're out on the Run," Cora said. "It absorbs your body temperature, temporarily shielding you from things like thermal imaging from drones and satellites.

"Very well put," Garnier said absently.

After the prepper finished applying the Ice Skin, another team member stepped forward and ran a metal detector loosely around Cora's body. The device also had a sensor to detect any kind of electrical signal stronger than the average output of a regular human being.

"No electronics, right?" Damius said, watching closely as they ran a similar detector around his body. "I heard about this on the way over."

"That's right," Garnier said, finally looking up from his notebook. "No electronics of any kind. Period."

"But, what if something happens to us?" Damius asked. "How do we get help when we're out there if we don't have any tools?"

Garnier's face turned to stone as Cora tried to resist awkwardly shuffling her feet.

"You're not in the military anymore, son," Garnier replied curtly. "There's no backup here. You run, or you die. It's as simple as that. Soka, what's the First Rule?"

"Never stop running," Soka replied. "Not even for your teammates."

"That's right," Garnier said. "*Never* stop running. If one of your teammates gets injured or killed, you don't stop. It's your duty to keep moving."

"Doesn't that defeat the point of the term *teammates*?" Damius asked. "We were taught never to abandon our unit. I don't leave soldiers behind, sir."

Garnier's eyes grew cold. "Then don't think of them as soldiers. In fact, don't even think of them as teammates if that makes it easier. The work we do here is too important to focus on any one life. Without us, the front wouldn't get the critical intel they need so desperately from Command Central. We're literally saving the world with the work we do. Cora, the Second Rule?"

"Don't deviate from the path," she said as if she were reciting a scripture.

"Self-explanatory," Garnier said, taking a few steps forward. "You do not deviate from the designated path in any way. That means if I say, 'run through the Devil's Trail,' you run through the Devil's Trail. That means if I ask you to go to hell and back, you do it. You got that, *greenleg*?"

Damius hesitated but nodded his head.

"Good," Garnier replied. "I apologize that you weren't given a formal orientation, but frankly, we're just scrambling to keep our ranks organized as it is. We need you striders out there delivering our messages as best you can. Hardok cyber technology has advanced so that it can intercept and decipher all of our net transmissions and radio signals. That's why we're here. The OLCs are the only effective way to send classified messages without the Hardoks knowing about it. They don't know about this program, and that's how we stay alive. We also stay alive by following the Three Rules. It's a ruthless system, but it's what's keeping all of our heads intact."

The white-uniformed personnel had paused during the conversation, so Garnier had to wave them back to continue their work. Three of the preppers stepped forward. Each one held a hollow metallic cylinder in their hands.

"These are what we call the Clamps," Garnier said.

"More like handcuffs," Cora mumbled. Garnier glanced at her, his face expressionless.

The preppers pressed a button on the Clamps, making the devices snap open on a hinge. The woman next to Cora grabbed her left wrist and slid the Clamp over her forearm, and snapped it shut with a click.

"Soka," Garnier said, "please explain what the Clamps are used for."

"The Clamps have three different compartments," Soka said in his thick accent. "The most important one is hidden. It contains the classified message we're transporting to the front. If it's opened without the correct key, a vial of acidic liquid floods the chamber, destroying it. The blue chamber," he said, tapping a small blue square on the Clamp, "contains ethol pills. One pill shoots bio-engineered adrenaline—among other chemicals—into your system that will keep you running for eight hours straight. There are three ethol pills total for most runs. Good enough for over twenty-four hours."

"And the red chamber?" Damius asked, pointing at the red circle on his Clamp.

"That's the nighty night," Soka responded. "Poison. If something happens on the run and you're incapacitated, or you get captured, you pop the nighty night and .... "

"Go into a long sleep," Damius said with a nod. "I get it. What's it made of?"

"That's classified," Garnier said sternly, not looking up.

Next, the preppers put a light backpack onto the backs of the three striders. Each bag had two tubes attached to the shoulder strap.

"The ethol pill isn't enough to keep you running for twenty-four hours straight," Soka said. "The bag is full of chai and water. When you're finished, the bag sucks the tube's contents back into the bag to keep it cool. The ethol pill will keep you from feeling thirsty, so make sure you drink more water than you think you need. You're going to be burning through calories like mad, so don't go skimpy on the chai either. Your body will need all the nutrients it can get."

"Well," Garnier said, putting both hands behind his back, "how's that for an orientation, son?"

"That's it?" Damius asked.

"Pretty much," Garnier replied. "All you need to do is run. Follow my rules, and you'll be just fine. Soka will be the team leader. New kid, you stick behind Soka, and Cora will take the rear. Understood?" He directed the question at all of them.

"Understood," Cora and Soka said in unison.

Garnier focused in on Damius. "Is that understood, son?"

Damius slowly nodded. "Understood, sir."

"Good," Garnier said, waving the preppers away. As the white-clad figures departed, Garnier stepped forward and opened the folder in his hand. Once he was sure all of the preppers had exited the chamber, he turned his attention back to the striders and said, "Your route will be west through the Devil's Trail and across Rigg's Crossing. Deliver the message in the Clamp to General Sheem at Harne's Skyforce Base. Repeat it back to me."

Cora had instantly memorized the instructions, but they had to repeat it back a few times until Damius got it totally right.

"All right then," Garnier said. "It's time to send you striders on your way. Once I open the Jaw, take your first ethol pill, and run like your lives depend on it. Any questions?"

Cora glanced to the side. It looked as if Damius wanted to ask a question, but he sufferingly remained silent.

"Very well then, striders," Garnier said as he snapped his folder shut. "Run like the devil *is* on your trail." Without another word, he spun on his heels and marched off the yellow platform and back into the Glass Room, closing the door with a resounding thud.

"What's so bad about the Devil's Trail?" Damius asked, directing his question at Soka. "What is everyone so afraid of?"

"You ask a lot of questions," Soka said.

"In my experience, you don't go into a battlefield without scouting it out first, planning a strategy."

"Look where that got you," Cora mumbled.

Both Damius and Soka paused, looking at her.

"What?" she asked with a shoulder shrug, her eyes narrow. Damius looked at her for a moment with cold gray eyes as he clutched his stump, but thankfully he didn't say anything.

"Go ahead, Cora," Soka said. "Tell him."

Cora sighed but said, "Many years ago, Arnonian military scientists used the Shamala Desert for chemical warfare testing."

"Chemical warfare?"

Cora nodded. "All of the villages in the vicinity were supposed to be evacuated before the testing. Unfortunately, one village was nestled in a valley that didn't get out before chemical bombs were dropped. Officially, this accident never took place."

"Are you worried about radiation then?" Damius asked.

"Not directly," Soka interjected. "Most of the radiation and chemical residue in the valley has dissipated over time. As long as you don't spend more than a day in the valley, you don't have to worry about radiation poisoning."

"Then what's out there exactly?" Damius asked.

Cora bristled at the question.

"Pitters," Soka replied.

Damius raised his eyebrows. "What?"

"Pitters," Soka repeated. "The residents of that ill-fated valley."

Damius narrowed his eyes at Soka. "What do these ... pitters look like?"

Soka shrugged. "Don't know, and I don't care to know. Cora is the only strider I know who has seen a pitter in person before."

Cora frowned. *Why did you have to bring that up, Soka?*

Damius turned and looked at her, his eyes expectant.

"Don't worry about the pitters," Cora mumbled, keeping her eyes on the steel floor. "As long as you stay away from the water pits, you'll survive."

Damius didn't respond.

"Hey, Damius," Soka said, gesturing at his Clamp to get the soldier's attention. "If you get lost or separated, there's a map on your Clamp." He raised his Clamp and pointed at the underside, where a printed map was kept underneath a plastic sleeve. "Just in case."

"Got it," Damius said.

Cora shook her head. It wasn't uncommon for striders to get separated from one another, but it never meant anything good when they did. If a strider got separated, they were most likely dead. That's just the way Runs were.

All three looked up at the ceiling when an alarm sounded, and an orange light began to flash near the giant gate. The yellow platform lurched upwards, throwing all three of the striders slightly off balance. The machine quickly stabilized and slowly raised them upwards towards the red-painted metal contraption above them.

"Time for the first ethol pill," Cora said. She pressed the blue button, and a pill popped into her hand. Cora flicked the pill into her mouth and took a swig of water from the tube on her shoulder, swallowing it in one gulp. She always did it quickly because the pill's outer coating tasted like coconut, which always made her gag. Soka followed suit, but Damius held the tablet silently in his hand.

"Go ahead," Soka said, wiping his mouth with his sleeve.

Damius hesitated but finally popped the pill into his mouth and swallowed with a swig of water.

"It's going to feel a little ... odd," Cora said, flexing her muscles in anticipation.

"Like what—" Damius coughed and lurched forward, his eyes wide as saucers. He managed to stay standing, but he looked like he was about to throw up.

Cora smiled. It was always fun to see greenlegs try their first ethol pill. She closed her eyes and clenched her fists as the effects of the tablet overcame her. For a moment, there was a brief flash of pain. Then it was instantly gone, replaced by a surging feeling that felt like her blood was flowing a thousand miles an hour inside her heart and arteries. The blood flow started from the bottom and rushed up through her body until it made it to her brain. She opened her eyes when it felt like her head was about to pop like a balloon. The lights in the metallic cavern seemed brighter than usual, and everything looked just a little sharper.

After a few seconds, she managed to take a deep breath and gain a sense of internal equilibrium once again as the ethol pill raged inside her like a storming ocean.

Soka had similarly just regained his composure. He reached out and slapped the hunched-over Damius on the back. "Come on, soldier boy. You're all right. Stand up."

Damius's eyes were still open wide in a look of excruciating pain, but he managed to pull himself upright. Just as he stood to his full height, the orange light above the Jaw turned red. The alarm instantly died, and a dread silence filled the steel chamber. And then, just as suddenly, the red gate cracked open. The red paint covering most of the ceiling was peeling off in patches, making the Jaw look like a gaping, bloody mouth. As the horizontal slit of the Jaw began to widen, the interlocking metal teeth of the door became visible. As it opened, it truly looked like they were standing in the mouth of a giant monster with terrifying metal chompers. The sight always made a shiver run down Cora's spine at the thought of being eaten alive by a metal beast.

The sun was directly overhead, beating down, and when Cora looked up, she had to cover her eyes with her hand.

"Whoa," Damius said. "I'm dizzy."

Cora looked down at the man beside her, who looked like he was nearly about to topple over. Before he had a chance to fall over, she grabbed his upper arm with both hands and kept him standing. "Come on, greenleg. You'll be fine."

They slowly continued ascending upwards until they passed the teeth of the Jaw. A vast expanse of blindingly white terrain opened up before them. The orange sun beat down on the hard ground, giving it a blinding glare that made Cora squint to see. The Arnen Flats were on the edge of the Shamala Desert. They would have to cross the barren landscape before coming to the Devil's Trail valley.

The yellow platform suddenly stopped without any warning, which threw the three off balance once again.

"Now what?" Damius said, pulling his arm out of Cora's grip.

"We run," Soka said. He stepped forward until he came to the platform's edge and stepped off onto the white sand.

Damius turned and looked at Cora. She returned his stare before motioning with her hand after Soka. "Your turn, greenleg. You're in the middle, remember?"

Damius still looked dazed, but he managed to nod his head before following Soka's lead.

As she watched the former soldier begin his first Run, Cora cocked her head in both directions as she always did. *Well, here you go,* she thought. *You got this. Don't think, just move.* Without looking back, she took off after the others who had already started running into the desolate, desert heat.

3

The Run

As she started to run, she heard the platform being lowered back into the facility behind her. A moment later, she could feel the rumble underneath her feet as the Jaw's gears screeched and the horizontal door began to close. After a few moments, it sealed together with a resounding thud.

Not too far ahead of her were Damius and Soka in the lead. Due to the energy boost of the ethol pill, Damius easily managed to keep up with Soka, who had set out at a steady pace across the sandy flats. The ethol pill didn't necessarily make them run faster than usual, but it would allow them to run at a faster speed for many more miles than was naturally possible without any sort of enhancement. After a Run, it took a good three weeks of rest and recuperation to fully recover from the strain it put on the human body.

Running in the sand was difficult, but with the ethol pill, Cora barely noticed the inconvenience. Her veins felt like lightning coursing through her, and she needed to move, to push her body to its limits.

The flat terrain turned to mountainous dunes, forcing Soka to begin altering his path as they ascended each rise as it came.

As they steadily made their way across the glaringly hot terrain, Cora found herself slipping into what she called the Focus. It came over her so naturally that she usually didn't even realize it happening until she was fully enveloped in it. Cora wasn't sure if it was the ethol pill altering her brain chemistry or just a survival technique of her mind. However, she suspected it had something to do with the tablet. In any case, it helped keep her sane during the arduous Runs.

Whatever the cause, the Focus was a mental state that blocked everything except the path directly before her. She knew that her eyes could physically see everything as usual. Still, the only image that her brain processed was the patch of land her next footstep was going to land on, then the next, and the next. Everything else was blocked out, removed. All she could think about was the next step and the thrill of moving her body to the beat of her pumping blood.

The sun overhead beat down on the three striders like it was shooting down arrows made of light rays. Cora could feel the sweat pouring off her body, soaking her tank-top. They didn't need any kind of sunscreen. The Ice Skin provided them with all the protection they needed. Not only did it shield them from the prying digital eyes of the Hardoks, but it also lent them resistance to the sun's rays. Under normal conditions, the beating sun would have customarily burnt their skin to crisps.

She couldn't be sure how long they had been running for—probably hours—when she realized that the terrain below her feet had changed. Gone were the sandy dunes, replaced with black rock and sandstone.

They were now entering the Devil's Trail.

The Valley of Sorrows.

She managed to pull herself out of the Focus just long enough to see black hills of rock rising up on either side of them, like stained teeth jutting up out of the ground. Based on her shadow's length, she calculated they had been running for twelve hours or more.

It had only felt like a few hours.

4

The Pitters

A t some point, they must have stopped to take their second ethol pills, but Cora couldn't even remember stopping. She was breathing heavily through her nose, but her muscles continued to pound away, step by step—mile by mile.

They took a bend in the trail. Cora knew it well. They would reach the old abandoned Errian ghost village in just a few more miles. *Well, not abandoned precisely,* she thought glumly to herself. Flashes of Marla seeped into her thoughts. Just as quickly as they came, Cora pushed them out. Thinking about Marla couldn't help her now. It would only distract her. Cora returned her full attention to the Run. *Maybe you keep running to push her out,* a distant voice seemed to say, echoing softly in the back of her mind. Cora pushed harder, focusing only on her breathing and footsteps to distract her from her mind. It seemed to work. The thoughts sufferingly vanished as she turned herself entirely over to the Focus. She would need all the—

An explosion of orange flames and loose dirt shot up into the air ahead of her. Soka was the one standing closest to the blast when it went off. He was thrown through the air, his body flailing like a rag doll. The impact hit Damius head-on, which sent him flying back like a cannonball. He collided with Cora, and they both tumbled to the ground. Cora's face got shoved into the loose sand, but luckily she missed any rocks from tearing her face open.

It took a moment for the Focus to leave her mind, so her survival instincts could kick in. Her ears were ringing, a pulsing buzz that made her head hurt. What happened? she wondered groggily, pushing herself up on all fours. Damius lay a short distance away, his chest heaving. His right leg lay beneath him at an awkward angle, broken. Probably a fracture.

Cora spit out the sand that had found itself into her mouth and looked around. A mangled heap lay not far from where the explosion had detonated. Cora tried to stand, but her legs were too wobbly to balance. She quickly stumbled over to Soka's ravaged body lying face down in the sand. She reached out and pulled the man over onto his back with both hands.

Cora threw her hand up over her mouth at the sight. Soka's body was burnt beyond recognition, chunks of his body and face blasted apart.

Dead.

A sick feeling erupted in the pits of Cora's stomach that tasted like a horrible aftertaste. She stumbled away from the corpse and wretched. She wiped her mouth with the back of her hand as her eyes fell on Damius, who was still back where he had been before. He was breathing but not moving. No sound came out of his mouth.

Never stop running, she heard a voice say in the back of her mind. *Leave him. He's dead anyway.*

This time, Cora successfully rose to her feet, though she was unsteady. She looked down at Damius for a moment before turning back to the trail. Cora took a half step but stopped. She turned and looked back at the soldier, then back at the path, then again back at the boy.

What are you doing? she thought, her body paralyzed by indecision. *Run! Leave him. You need to follow the rules; get the Clamp safely to the Skyforce. Move!* She took another half step and was about to break out into a run, but something stopped her. *Marla.*

Cora stopped.

Marla.

Before she fully knew what she was doing, she ran back to the soldier and knelt beside him. Luckily, the blast had only singed his face and clothes, so he was otherwise unhurt aside from his leg.

"Hey, hey!" she said, snapping her fingers above his closed eyelids. "Hey, stupid, wake up."

No response.

She grabbed his shoulders in frustration and shook him hard. Thankfully his eyelids fluttered, and he managed to utter, "Tamra?" He spoke deliriously. "Is that you? What are you ... doing here?"

Cora groaned. "Come on, city boy. We have to go."

Damius didn't say anything as she helped him into a sitting position.

"I ... I can't feel my leg," he said.

"Trust me, you will momentarily," Cora replied. She put one of his arms around her shoulder and hoisted him up. He screamed.

"Shh!" Cora hissed. "You've felt pain before. Toughen up."

Damius acted like he wanted to say something, but he couldn't quite get it out.

"Come on, we've got to move," Cora said. "Maybe we'll find something to splint your leg up with along the way."

They took a hesitant step forward, Damius hopping on his one good leg, jaw clenched.

"Good, good," Cora said. "At this rate, we'll be there in two months." Damius ignored her.

They managed a dozen more steps. Cora glanced over at Soka's body, which was laying peacefully beside the trail. *Goodbye, Soka. I'm so, so sorry.*

It was slow-moving. Each small step they managed felt like a victory, but Cora knew full well that with Damius's injury, they weren't going to make good time. At the rate they were moving, it would be well into the next evening when they would arrive at the Skyforce base if they made it that far. For now, they just needed to get to the village that was only a few bends up ahead. The buildings weren't visible yet, but they would be soon.

As they got closer, Damius managed to blurt out, "Er ... Errian."

"What?" Cora asked, keeping her eyes peeled forward.

"That ... was an Errian landmine," Damius said with some difficulty.

"Errian?"

Damius nodded fervently.

"I didn't think any of them were left," Cora said. "Not after ... the tests. Not after what happened here."

"I didn't know until today why they had left in the first place," Damius said, "but now it all makes sense. The ones that survived the chemical weapons fled to Hardok controlled territory, where they found refuge. The Hardoks have been using Errian warriors as trackers and hunters ... sometimes even assassins. I don't know what they call themselves, but we call them Ghostovs."

"Ghostovs?"

"Yeah, you know, like the urban legend?" The more Damius talked, the more it seemed to take his mind off the pain, if only somewhat. "Have you ever run into minefields out here before?"

Cora shook her head. "Never. Are you saying one of these Ghostov killers is running around out here planting mines?"

"Not running around," Damius said. "*Hunting.*"

"How do you know about all of this?"

Damius raised his stump of an arm. "I've gotten too close before. If a Ghostov is out here, that means the Hardoks know about the OLCs. They must have figured out how the United Front was communicating."

Cora looked ahead. The clay buildings of the Errian ghost town suddenly came into view. Just a few more steps and they would arrive. In just a half-hour, the sun would be set entirely. They had to be out of this area before that time, or the pitters—

Cora pushed the thought out of her mind. She couldn't think about *that*. The talk about the Ghostov frightened her, but nothing could compare with the fear she felt from the creatures that roamed the desert at night. They just had to move forward without stopping. If they took too long to make it past the Errian village, they would end up as pitter food.

Just in time to confirm her fears, she spotted a water pit a short distance ahead of them, its diameter about five feet wide. The water was so dark it was almost black. Two hollow reeds stuck up out of the pit, slowly rocking back and forth in the muddy water, causing slight ripples on the surface.

"Is that—?"

"Shh!" Cora hissed. "Don't speak. Pitters can't hear you, but they can feel vibrations. Don't stop moving. We have to get past this place before the sun goes down."

Damius's soldierly instincts kicked in. His body somehow became more tense and rigid than before, his eyes alert. As they passed the pit, they gave it as wide a berth as possible, but it was still uncomfortably close for Cora's tastes. They both eyed the pool of water as they passed by. The two reeds continued swaying in the water, back and forth.

Cora sighed in relief as they passed, but just as soon as they rounded the first pit, a second came into view, then a third, and a fourth. There would be a whole series of water pits surrounding them as they passed through the forgotten village. Each hole ranged from one reed to four. A few of the pits had no reeds, which was a good sign. Only the pits with reeds had pitters hidden underneath the calm surface. They were waiting, feeling the vibrations in the earth of the intruders up above.

But they wouldn't emerge, at least not yet.

As they passed the third pit, they came upon the first clay building that had lain dormant for twenty years or more. The clay structures were round, with large bricks making up the walls with clay and straw rooftops. Most of the rooftops had caved in, though the sturdy walls all remained intact.

They remained silent as they moved farther into the desolate ruins, their footsteps echoing off the canyon walls around them. Cora looked up. The sun was getting dangerously close to setting.

They needed to hurry.

"Pick up the pace," Cora whispered, taking a deep breath.

Damius gritted his teeth and nodded his head, trying to push back the pain.

The village didn't have roads, just a meandering trail that snaked back and forth. They started weaving through the buildings, moving faster than they had before, though it still felt too slow. Water pits continued to dot the land around them, though most of the water holes inside the village didn't have reeds.

Cora kept her eyes nervously on the setting sun. It seemed to grow larger in size as the air pollutants made it look more majestic than it really was.

Long shadows fell over the village.

They were running out of time.

5

The Ruins

They moved a little bit quicker, the fading light a stark indicator of their dire position. After a few moments, they finally saw the end of the clay buildings. *Almost there,* Cora thought.

They came up to another pit with a single reed sticking up out of it. Just as they were about to move around it, Damius stumbled, which pulled Cora down, almost to her knees. A split second later, a projectile whizzed above Cora's head and hit a clay jar sitting outside one of the brick huts. Before Cora had a chance to process what had just happened, a skeletal hand shot up out of the water pit and snatched her ankle. She tripped and fell, Damius collapsing beside her. She looked down with horror to see an unnaturally long arm snaking out of the water pit, clutching her ankle with a death grip. The limb was made entirely of bone, sinew, and naked muscle.

Damius grabbed at his belt and withdrew a long silver knife. As Cora struggled against the pitter's clawed hand to no avail, Damius lunged forward. In one fell swoop with his long knife, he severed the hand from the lanky arm. A strange scream emanated from out of the pit, but the arm snaked back into the murky surface, disappearing from view.

"The Ghostov!" Damius said, speaking as loudly as he could without shouting.

Cora nodded vigorously in agreement. She stood to her feet and dragged Damius up with her. She looked up once again. Just a sliver of sunlight remained.

"Stay low," Damius said, doing his best to crouch. "The Ghostov has us in his sights. That was a sniper round. He's up in those hills somewhere behind us. Move!"

He shoved her towards the nearest building without waiting for her to respond. Cora stumbled forward but froze. "We can't ... we can't stay here! We need to get out of this canyon."

"Go!" Damius ordered, beads of sweat pouring down his face, his jaw clenched in pain as he sat on one knee. Damius shoved her once more just as another bullet narrowly whipped past her head.

This snapped Cora out of her trance-like state. She reached back and pulled Damius forward. Together they stumbled towards the nearest structure and burst through the wooden door that screeched on rusted hinges. Damius collapsed onto the stone ground as Cora turned back towards the doorway.

The sunlight was gone.

The village was now fully encompassed in shadow.

She grasped the edge of the door and stood in petrified horror as a gangly skeletal shape slowly started to crawl out of the nearest mud pit, its elbows akin to a spider's legs. Eyeless sockets stared back at her. Without waiting for the pitter to fully emerge, she slammed the door shut and put her back to it, breathing heavily. "We're dead," she whispered between breaths. "We're so dead."

"Not yet, we're not," Damius responded through clenched teeth.

"Well, if the Ghostov assassin doesn't blow our brains out, then the pitters might just eat them," Cora said.

"One problem at a time," Damius said, looking around.

To accentuate his point, something slammed against the other side of the door. The force knocked Cora a few inches forward. She slammed her weight back against the door. The frame and hinges weren't going to last long before it busted down altogether.

"It's a *pretty big* problem," she hissed back.

"Is there a way out of here?" Damius asked, looking around frantically.

Cora's mind raced as she looked around in the darkened room. There were no windows, and the only door was the one she was guarding. Then suddenly, a history lesson from school popped into her head. "The Errian's had a sewage system in their village!"

Damius gave her a look that said, *'How could you possibly know that?'* but without asking any questions, he stumbled over to a stubby clay cylinder poking up out of the floor. It appeared to be a crude toilet seat of some sort at second glance. Damius reached up with his good leg and kicked. The toilet barely budged.

The pitter smashed into the door once again. "Hurry, Damius!"

He kicked again. It moved an inch. With his third kick, the clay toilet toppled over, revealing a hole in the ground. "Come on!"

"You go first!" Cora said. "Someone needs to hold the door."

Damius didn't argue. Headfirst, he slipped into the hole in the ground. A moment later, he vanished from sight.

Sweat poured down Cora's face. She couldn't move, not yet. She had to wait for one more attack.

"Cora?" Damius yelled from down in the sewage tunnel. "Come on!"

Not yet, she thought. *Wait ....* Time seemed to tick on at an unbearable rate. She couldn't hear anything outside the door. Was the pitter gone?

She jumped when the door was hit so hard the top hinge broke loose. *Now or never.* Without waiting for another attack, Cora leaped forward. She slid on the ground straight towards the sewage hole, scraping her arms and elbows in the process.

She crawled into the hole with the grace of a flopping fish, head first after Damius' example. She panicked when she realized she wasn't sure how deep the hole went. Before she could pull herself out, she slipped and fell straight down.

She wanted to scream, but her stomach clenched up so tight she could barely breathe. She fell onto something soft. It was Damius. He grimaced in pain, but before Cora could say anything, he slapped a hand over her mouth.

They lay breathing in silence for a moment in an awkward tangle before Damius slowly took his hand away. It had felt like dozens of feet, but the drop was only five or six feet down in reality. It was totally dark. She could only see the faint outline of Damius as they lay together in the cramped space. Luckily the sewer had dried up years ago. All that remained was a foul stench that nearly made Cora want to puke all over the soldier boy.

They both looked up when they heard a *bang*. The door crashed down, and a lumbering sound slowly started shuffling around on the ground level above them. Cora and Damius kept totally still, eyes peeled towards the surface.

A shadow flickered above them, illuminated by a ray of moonlight.

More footsteps.

Silence. Silence.

Shuffling.

The stillness persisted. Cora heard something that sounded far away, but it was hard to tell inside the sewage tunnel. *Is it gone?*

They waited.

It felt like hours, but Cora was sure it had only been minutes. Her heart was still beating as if a mad drummer had taken over her circulation system. Adrenaline still pulsed through her body from the ethol pill, keeping her alert. Damius slowly moved his head to look at her. Her eyes were slowly adjusting to the darkness, and she could barely see his facial gestures. He seemed to be asking, *Is it gone?*

Cora shrugged her shoulders, taking care not to move too much or too quickly. They continued to wait. Shrieks began to sound off in the distance. Cora had seen a pitter once before, but not at night. She wasn't sure what to expect. Did the pitters just wander around like mindless monsters, howling at the moon? It seemed—

An arm suddenly lunged out of the darkness above them and reached down into the sewage pipe, scratching and scraping at the sides in a wild frenzy. It was all Cora could do not to shriek in surprise. She felt Damius's body tense up at the pitter's sudden attack, who had clearly not left the building above. The skeletal hand was only a foot above Cora's head as it scratched and clawed around the edge of the pipe, almost as if it was looking for something.

Suddenly, the pitter forced its shoulder into the hole as its arm stretched downward. The clawed fingers were just an inch or two away from Cora's hair. She wanted to scream, but instinctively, she forced her body to go completely still. She couldn't breathe. A knot formed in Cora's stomach. It tightened like she was being strangled from the inside out. She almost jumped out of her skin when she felt a fingertip brush along a few outcropping strands of hair. With only her eyes, she looked desperately into Damius' eyes. He subtly shook his head, and in her mind, she could hear his voice saying, *'Don't move a muscle.'*

After a moment, the pitter's fingertip moved on and continued clawing at another section of the pipe. After another minute, the arm slowly receded and disappeared. The pitter stumbled to its unsteady feet and shuffled away. They could hear the monster as it walked away, exiting the building.

Only once she was positive the pitter was gone did Cora exhale.

They sat in silence, not moving. Haunting sounds continued in the world above them. Sudden shrieks echoed through the pipe every couple of minutes.

It had felt like an eternity when Damius finally whispered, "Are you okay?" His voice was so low Cora almost couldn't understand what he had asked.

Cora could only nod in response. She finally forced her insides to relax enough to be able to speak. "That was a close shave."

Damius nodded. They sat in silence for a while longer. Shrieks from above filled the cramped air. There were more of them out there than before.

"Why did you join the OLCs?" Damius asked from out of nowhere.

Cora turned to look at him. "What?"

"Why did you become a strider?"

"What are you talking about?"

"It's just that ... " Damius licked his lips. " ... It's just that you don't seem to like being a sprinter. You don't even do it out of a sense of duty or anything like that. You force yourself to do it."

"Are you just trying to get me to talk?" Cora asked. "Take my mind off of the cannibalistic monsters and native assassins?"

Damius nodded. "Maybe."

"I—" she paused. "I don't really know what to say."

Damius didn't respond. He just let the silence linger in the cramped air.

Cora licked her lips. "I used to be a biochemical major at Hardstrom University." Just that thought put a slight smile onto her face. It had been a long time since she had even thought about her higher education days. "I love science. Always have. My Father works for Biolonic. I guess I took after him. He was the dreamer. My Mom stayed home to raise my brother and me, but she wasn't an ordinary housewife. She's a killer, but not in the literal sense. She's the strongest person I know."

Damius still didn't say anything back, but he had relaxed.

"My brother, Rimes, took after my Mom, I guess. Rimes's always been a fighter. It was always his dream to join the United Front. That was everything he focused on. Even though he wasn't that good in school, he pushed himself to be the best student he could be, especially for the classes that would get him a good score for the Hardith Academy. He graduated at the top of his class. They used to think that he had supernatural powers or something because he ate and slept there, killing himself at night doing everything he possibly could. He was one of the best cadets they had ever seen. At least if my Mother's stories are to be believed, anyway.

"He hadn't yet graduated when the war broke out. He quickly ended up as a Scout, stationed out in the hills north of Vardover City. From what we gathered, his unit received instruction to push out towards the west. They knew that Hardok heavy infantry units had been spotted in the area, but they followed orders. What they didn't realize was that the Hardoks knew about their position and .... "

Cora trailed off. She glanced at Damius, but his face remained blank. "Turns out that a team of striders failed to get a message delivered in time that would have drastically changed the United Front's intel on the area. That one mistake—" She let out a heavy breath. "But that's why I became a strider. Once I heard the news, I couldn't focus anymore. I used to run track, even though I wasn't very good. I dropped out of school and joined the OLCs. So ... yeah."

"I know it doesn't mean much coming from me, but I'm sorry," Damius whispered. "I've got two younger brothers of my own."

Cora felt like crying, but her face remained dry. It seemed that she had already cried herself dry a long time ago.

They lapsed into silence as the howls of the pitters echoed above them.

27

"Who's Marla?" Damius asked, once again abruptly breaking the silence.

Cora looked at him with wide eyes. "What did you say?"

"Marla," Damius replied. "You kept saying her name under your breath when you dragged me here. Who is she?"

Cora slumped back against the pipe wall, her face going hard. Her eyes darted back and forth. It had been hard enough talking about Rimes; she couldn't even think about talking about Marla and her unexpected death.

Damius sensed that she didn't want to talk about Marla, so he went silent.

Cora looked up at the cusp of the pipe, her eyes narrow. The haunting shrieks from the pitters continued up above. Eventually, sunrise would come upon them, and the skinless creatures would retreat into their pits. At that time, their only threat would be the Ghostov, who was waiting for them, watching. *But will he try to pick us off from afar before we can escape into the canyon, or will he try to come in close, deal with us up close and personal?* From what Damius had said about Ghostovs, either option was bad news.

But for now, all they could do was wait.

6

The Ghostov

Cora woke with a start. It took her a moment to realize where she was. Her cramped muscles quickly reminded her. *We're still in the pipe.* She still sat atop Damius, who was awake and alert, their bodies entangled together. Damius's eyes were cast upwards, staring at the hole's rim.

"The pitters are beginning to retreat," he whispered, not taking his eyes off the cusp. "It'll be sunrise in twenty minutes."

Cora yawned, though she tried to squelch it. She could still hear distant sounds of moaning and shuffling feet.

"He's out there."

Cora paused. "The Ghostov?"

Damius looked down and locked eyes with her. "Without weapons, we're no match for him."

"You've got a knife," Cora said.

"They're guerrilla fighters; assassins," Damius said. "They're dangerous from a distance, but they're absolute devils when they get close."

"What do you think he's going to do?" Cora asked.

"Push his advantage," Damius replied. "Take us out by hand. He's not going to risk us getting to the canyon where he knows he could possibly lose us. He'll take us out as quickly as possible once the pitters are gone."

Silence.

"What are we going to do?" Cora asked.

Damius slowly shook his head. "I don't know."

The reality of their impending death suddenly loomed over Cora. Not in a way that made her panic, but in the way that made her reflect. Surprisingly, she wasn't afraid, just worried. "She was my friend, you know."

Damius looked at her, his eyes searching.

"You know, striders aren't the friendliest of people, right?" she said softly. "Marla was different." She and Marla had never talked about being friends. They just ... *were*. Marla had felt more like a sister than anything else in many ways. "We used to talk about ice cream, boys, school, and ... everything. I think in a way, she literally helped save my life after—"

"Rimes?" Damius's stare reflected her own.

"It seems that anyone who dies in my life dies from a simple mistake. Marla was an amazing strider. She never complained and always finished her Runs. Always. But on one of our runs together, we were passing through this exact same village when it was time to take the ethol pill. Marla popped the pill, swallowed it, and continued running. A moment later, she collapsed. This was during the middle of the afternoon. I knew I shouldn't, but I stopped and ran back to her. I quickly realized what had happened. Somehow, one of the preppers had accidentally put a nighty night pill into one of her ethol pill canisters. Since you're supposed to chew the nighty night, I thought that if I could get her to throw the pill up, then maybe she could survive."

"What happened?" Damius's eyes were intense as he stared at her.

"The unthinkable happened," Cora said, her voice low. "I saw a blur, and then something had Marla by the leg. With unthinkable force, it pulled Marla out of my reach. At first, I thought it was a snake or some other kind of animal. It wasn't until it was dragging her away through the mud that I realized what it was."

"A pitter," Damius said, realization hitting him. "A pitter killed your friend."

Something welled up in Cora's throat that made it hard to talk. A shiver ran through her body. "I can still remember the look on her face when she went into the pit."

Damius looked deep in thought. "It was daytime, right? If pitters only come out at night, why did it emerge for Marla?"

Cora locked eyes with him. The question kind of struck her in a way that she didn't expect. Why *did* the pitter kill her? "I don't know exactly," she replied. "At first, I thought that maybe she had wandered too close to a pit, but then I concluded that when she collapsed, the vibration in the ground must have drawn one of the pitters out."

Damius seemed to consider this for a moment before shaking his head. "That doesn't make any kind of sense," he said slowly. "If pitters can feel the vibrations in the ground, then striders running through the Devil's Trail should bring them out every time we come this way. I don't think that someone collapsing would cause that reaction from the pitters. There has to be something else."

"Maybe they can sense when someone is vulnerable physically," Cora replied. "No one's ever collapsed like that so close to one of those pits."

"I don't think that's it," Damius replied. He looked like he was about to say more, but he paused and looked up. Cora followed suit when she realized what he was listening for.

Silence.

There were no more shrieks and wails of pain, no more shuffling of naked feet. The pitters had retreated back into their sanctuaries of water and mud. The village was empty, exposed.

"We have to get out of here, fast!" Damius said. "We can't let the Ghostov find us here. I'll help push you up."

Cora didn't argue. It was awkward trying to find any purchase inside of the narrow pipe. Still, with the help of Damius pushing her up from below, she managed to reach up and grab the lip of the hole with both hands. Damius used his hands to push her feet up, which helped her clamber the rest of the way out. She glanced around the empty hut. It was still dark, but she could see the world brightening up outside through the open doorframe.

She turned and lay prone next to the sewage pipe. She reached in with her right hand and said, "Hey, grab on!" She couldn't see him, but she felt Damius grasp her wrist. She pulled with everything she had until Damius managed to grip the rim of the pipe. Cora grabbed his backpack and helped pull him out the rest of the way. His face was grimaced with the pain from his leg, but he didn't groan or complain.

"I think I need a shower after that," Cora said as she helped Damius to his feet, putting his arm around her neck. "No, I *definitely* need a shower after that."

"I could have told you as much," Damius said, a small smile appearing through his pain-stricken face.

"Did you just tell a joke, soldier-boy?" Cora asked. "Maybe you're delirious."

"Oh, hilarious," he said. "Come on!"

They both shuffled over to the doorframe and were about to burst out into the cold morning air when a bullet zipped past their faces and burrowed into the clay wall on the hut's right side. They both lurched back inside, almost falling backward.

"He's still in the hills!" Cora said as she pulled Damius to the left.

"No," Damius said. "He's here in the village. That wasn't a rifle round. That was from a hand rod. He's close."

"What are we going to do?" Cora said, trying to keep herself from panicking.

Damius didn't reply. He pulled his knife out of the sheath on his belt. "Now that he's confirmed our location, he's not going to wait for us to come out again. He's going to storm the place."

Cora looked down at the blade in Damius' hand. A ray of sunlight glinted off the silvery edge from the rising sun shining through the doorway. She then looked at the broken door that lay on the ground in front of them. Without saying a word, she let Damius go and reached down to pull the door up on its side before dragging it to the back of the hut.

"What are you doing?" Damius asked, hopping on his good foot.

Cora positioned the door vertically to act as a blockade while keeping it in the sunlight. She leaned it up against the curved wall so it would stand on its own. "Get behind this," she said, rushing over to help Damius move. "When the Ghostov comes in, you can use your knife to reflect the sunlight to temporarily blind him."

"Might work," Damius said as Cora helped him over behind the vertical door. "But what are you going to do?"

After helping position Damius behind the door, Cora looked around. "I haven't thought that far ahead yet."

"Grab one of those loose bricks," Damius said, pointing with his knife at a deteriorating wall. "If I can stun him for long enough, smash his head in with it from the side while he's distracted with me."

Cora stumbled over to the wall and grabbed a loose brick, and twisted and tugged on it until it came loose in her hand. She turned and looked for the best position to hide. A clay fireplace was positioned up against the wall not too far from the door. It wouldn't offer her very good cover, but hopefully, she wouldn't be the first thing the Ghostov would see when he came through the doorway.

"Cora," Damius said.

Cora was shaking, but she glanced at Damius. His eyes were narrow, full of concern.

"Be careful," he said. "If you have a chance to run, do it. Don't stay for me."

Cora shook her head. "I'm not leaving you."

Damius returned her stare for a few moments before silently turning his attention back to the doorway.

They waited. A slight breeze was blowing outside the hut, making the dry grass rustle. Each noise made Cora sink farther back into the brick wall, but no Ghostov appeared. There were no gunshots, no footsteps, nothing.

Cora's body began to ache. Sitting in the sewage pipe for the whole night had left her sore in places that had never been sore before. Not only that, but she was also growing more anxious by the second. *How long can we wait?* she wondered.

Damius must have sensed her restlessness because he whispered, "Stay put."

Cora took a deep breath but continued to wait, brick in hand. It wasn't a good weapon, but maybe she could get close enough to crush the Ghostov's skull in. They would only have one chance—

She nearly jumped when she heard a sound outside the front door. It sounded like a resounding thump, like a leather drum. She raised the brick in her hand, her knuckles going white. Damius stirred on the other side of the hut, raising his knife.

She cast her eyes back towards the doorway. The light still shone through, but there were no more sounds. Cora could hear every breath in her lungs like a hammer striking an anvil. She—

Without warning, an explosion blew up the hut's back wall, which rained chunks of clay and shrapnel inside. The blast hit Damius in the back, throwing him to the ground. His knife clattered harmlessly away from his reach. One of the brick chunks struck Cora in the left leg, which made her drop to her knees, a flash of pain shooting through her. She looked up, teeth gritted. The backside of the hut was blown away with light streaming through the dust. It became all too clear. While they were waiting, the Ghostov had distracted them from the front while planting a bomb at the back.

Damius was already crawling along the ground, trying to reach his knife, when a shadowy figure appeared in the gaping hole. Cora could only stare in shock at the sight. A lanky man garbed in sandy white cloth wrapped around his body in layers stood there. His head was bald, which focused the attention on his dark eyes that were narrow and focused. Scars covered every inch of his skin and not the kind you get by accident. These scars were some kind of tribal markings. A long rifle wrapped in brown leather was slung over his shoulder, a hand rod clasped to his belt. But the thing that drew Cora's attention the most was the severed arm that hung off of the man's belt, a Clamp attached to the dismembered forearm.

Soka's arm.

Cora wanted to scream, but she found she couldn't move. In an instant, the Ghostov jumped into the hut and kicked the knife away from Damius' grasp. Damius tried to reach for the Ghostov's leg to trip him, but the pale man kicked again, smashing his boot into the soldier's face. The force of the kick knocked Damius onto his back, where he lay, possibly dead.

The brick! Cora thought. She hoisted the brick above her head and stood, pain shooting through her leg. She was about to strike when the Ghostov turned. His hand snapped out and grasped Cora's throat. She had never felt such strength before. It felt like fingers of iron were wrapped around her jugular.

The Ghostov raised his arm up and lifted Cora right off the ground. Cora's eyes went wide as she struggled in the man's grip, inadvertently dropping the brick in her hand. She tried kicking the Ghostov, but he stood firm, the kicks bouncing off him like she was kicking a boulder.

The Ghostov stared at her, his face emotionless. "You are weak," he said. His accent was thick, hard to understand. Even when he wasn't talking, his mouth hung open, almost as if he breathed through his mouth, not his nose. "I already take one arm. Perhaps I will take other, hm? Perhaps two more arm?" The Ghostov smiled as he reached for a knife hilt on his belt with his free hand, not looking away from Cora.

Cora's eyes bulged. She was going to die. The Ghostov was going to kill her and take her arm, or would he take her arm first before killing her?

"You people," the Ghostov said, slurring his words, "easy to kill. Like babies. Your arms will be mine. Tokens of victory."

Suddenly a thought came into Cora's mind. *Arms?* She couldn't move her head, but she managed to look down at the Clamp that was wrapped around her left forearm. *Of course!* she thought. The realization hit her like a bolt of lightning. *The pitter didn't come after Marla because she fell!* Cora thought. *Damius was right. It didn't have anything to do with vibrations or sounds. It's one of the pills!*

Just then, Cora knew what she had to do.

"I choke you out like baby chicken," the Ghostov continued. "Or I take arm first, hm? Let you bleed? Maybe I—"

Before the Ghostov had a chance to say anything else, Cora raised her arms. She hit the red button on the Clamp, releasing the nighty night pill, which popped into her open hand. The Ghostov's eyes went wide. Cora shoved her hand forward, palm outward, straight into the Ghostov's open mouth. She kicked her right knee up into the bottom of the man's chin, closing it shut with the nighty night pill inside.

The Ghostov's eyes went wide with surprise and shock as he dropped Cora to the ground. She fell to her knees and instantly began crawling desperately over to Damius. When she reached him, she cast a glance back at the Ghostov who was stumbling towards her, his hands clutching his throat, red foam bubbling out of his lips.

"You think you kill me?" the Ghostov said, hate burning in his eyes. He spit the red foam out onto the clay ground. "I survive worse as child. I kill you quick. You—"

Cora screeched when a sinewy form of bone and patchy flesh appeared in the hole of the back wall. Without hesitation, the pitter raced past her straight at the Ghostov. Cora threw her body protectively over Damius though there was no need. The pitter ignored her entirely as it rushed towards the Ghostov, its raw skin rippling in the sunlight. Another pitter shot in from the back of the hut, and then another. The Ghostov screamed as the pitters collapsed on top of him, tackling him to the ground. The three pitters quickly got hold of the Ghostov and pulled him towards the hole in the backside wall of the hut. His eyes wild, the Ghostov reached out with both hands and grabbed the brick wall. He screamed as the pitters pulled. The brick gave and broke free, and then the Ghostov was gone.

The Ghostov's screams from outside the hut were so fierce it felt like they could shatter glass. And then, complete silence as the Ghostov met a watery grave.

Cora looked down at Damius, whose eyes were thankfully cracked open.

"What ... what happened?"

"I just saved our lives, dummy," Cora said.

Damius coughed. "I feel like someone kicked me in the head."

"Stop whining," Cora said, pulling Damius groggily to his feet. "We've got a Run to finish."

Epilogue

They had whisked Damius away as soon as they had both reached the Skyforce Base. It wasn't until the next day that she learned that they had loaded Damius up into a B-130 airstream jet to get him proper medical attention. She would likely never see or speak to Damius again. They didn't even have a chance to say goodbye.

After she had finished her briefing, she learned that the nighty night pills were partially made from the same compound used in the chemical testing of the Errian territory. That was why the pitters were attracted to the things. The OLC Correspondent at the Skyforce Base assured her that they would stop using the nighty night tablets immediately. Cora wasn't so sure that the change would be made. The thing that the higher-ups were most interested in was the Ghostov. Luckily, with the Ghostov dead, he could not report back to his people. That meant that the OLC operations still had a green light, at least for now.

In the meantime, all Cora had to do was wait. She hated every moment of it.

It wasn't until days later that the siren sounded off outside her room. She nearly jumped off her cot before running outside into the long corridor underneath the base's main complex. This time, she was the first one in the small cart with the orange light. Two other striders sauntered out of their rooms before climbing in after her. One of the striders she recognized, though she couldn't remember his name. The other girl was a stranger.

After they were all situated, Cora looked at the girl who was not making eye contact and asked, "Greenleg?"

"What?" the young woman asked, looking up.

"Is this your first Run?"

The greenleg nodded.

"Don't worry, greenleg," Cora said. "I've got your back."

About the Author

Brett Seegmiller is an avid science fiction and fantasy reader and always dreamed of becoming a writer. He served a mission in Auckland, New Zealand, for The Church of Jesus Christ of Latter-Day Saints, an experience that profoundly impacted his ambition for writing and storytelling. Brett currently lives in Payson, Utah, with his wife and family, who inspire him every day.

You can connect with me on:
- https://www.brettseegmiller.com
- https://twitter.com/BrettSeegmiller
- https://www.facebook.com/brettcseegmiller

Made in the USA
Middletown, DE
15 January 2025

68776850R00071